Shatter The Dark

Jenna Collett

Copyright © 2021 Jenna Collett

All rights reserved

The characters and events portrayed in this book are fictitious. Any similarity to real persons, living or dead, is coincidental and not intended by the author.

No part of this book may be reproduced, or stored in a retrieval system, or transmitted in any form or by any means, electronic, mechanical, photocopying, recording, or otherwise, without express written permission of the publisher.

ISBN: 9798736387366
Imprint: Independently published

Edited by: Bryony Leah
https://www.bryonyleah.com/
Printed in the United States of America

Contents

Title Page
Copyright
Chapter 1 — 1
Chapter 2 — 12
Chapter 3 — 21
Chapter 4 — 30
Chapter 5 — 39
Chapter 6 — 48
Chapter 7 — 57
Chapter 8 — 66
Chapter 9 — 78
Chapter 10 — 87
Chapter 11 — 97
Chapter 12 — 107
Chapter 13 — 119
Chapter 14 — 131

Chapter 15	142
Chapter 16	154
Chapter 17	167
Chapter 18	176
Chapter 19	183
Chapter 20	191
Chapter 21	201
Chapter 22	210
Chapter 23	221
Chapter 24	229
Chapter 25	238
Chapter 26	251
Chapter 27	260
Thank you!	273
Books In This Series	275

Chapter 1

Liana

The witch was on the move.

Footsteps creaked down the hallway, and I tensed as a thin shaft of light spread beneath the doorframe. She paused outside the door, a looming presence that sent an icy shiver down my back. I held my breath, not making a sound, for fear she would enter. A long moment passed before I heard her footsteps resume and disappear deeper into the house.

The light vanished with her, and I squeezed my eyes shut, trying to hold onto the faint glow in my mind. But it didn't last. It never did.

Waves of dry heat flooded the vents inside our room, and the scent of woodsmoke clung to my clothes—a constant due to the roaring hearth the witch never let die down. Somewhere in the dark, my brother shifted his lanky frame, scuffing the dirty floor.

"Do you have any requests?" he asked.

I swallowed around the lump in my throat and opened my eyes. "The one father used to sing to us before bedtime when we were kids."

Hendrik sighed. "You always pick that one."

"It's my favorite."

"Mine too," he said, his tone laced with the longing of our shared memory.

He cleared his throat and whistled the familiar tune. The haunting notes hung in the air, grounding me in the pitch-black cell. Soon, the tight ache in my chest loosened, and my thoughts wandered to happier times. They felt like a lifetime ago. Before the money ran out, followed quickly by the food. Before our father left to find work in the mines and never returned.

We were forced out of our home, Hendrik barely sixteen. I had just turned fifteen. The streets didn't welcome us. After all, we were simply another pair of impoverished teenagers, scrambling for scraps among gaunt faces that looked just like ours.

For a while, we made it work. Hendrik picked up odd jobs where he could, and I sold what was left of our meager belongings on the street. But when Hendrik injured his leg in an accident and could no longer work, we became desperate.

That was when I met her.

"Hendrik?"

The whistling stopped.

I pressed my face against the metal bars of our cell, feeling the warm rust scrape my skin. "How many days?"

"One day, Liana. Only one day until we're free."

"We'll escape tomorrow then," I said, releasing the

bars to sit cross-legged on the floor. My brother always made the same promise, but this time, I believed it might be true.

I had a plan.

Hendrik restarted his tune, and I relaxed to the pleasant sound. Reaching into my pocket, I closed my fingers around a small peppermint candy. My pockets were full of hardened bars of sugar, courtesy of the witch. The sweet mints were laced with something that made time blur, and tonight, we wouldn't be eating them.

There was only one way to escape. The witch always delivered our food before dawn. We'd wake up groggy to a bowl of cold gruel and a hunk of crusty bread sitting against the wall. Yesterday, I watched her leave the key in the lock while she placed our meal.

We needed that key.

It was risky, but it was our only chance. Once she realized we had stopped eating her candies, there was no telling what she'd do, and I was afraid she'd separate us.

Even without the mints, the heat made me drowsy. I lay down on the rough floorboards to wait. There was always so much time to think. To wonder why we were here. To dream about being anywhere else.

I must have dozed off, because I awoke when the cell door whined on its rusty hinge. Peeking through half-closed eyes, I kept my breathing even, feigning the deep sleep the witch expected. She placed a lantern on the floor and lowered a tray of food to the ground. My body coiled with tension as she turned her back. I started to count, ready to spring for the door with the key still inserted in the lock.

One…two…thr—

The witch tilted her head as if she could hear my intentions. I went still, my heart racing, as she moved closer. Light from the lantern illuminated her craggy face. Her eyes were two chips of coal set above harsh cheekbones.

What was she doing? Did she know I planned to escape?

She stopped beside me and leaned over, whispering something unintelligible. The tips of her stringy gray hair brushed against my shoulder. She smelled of mothballs and decaying earth, combined with something that wasn't tangible, but could only be described as sinister.

I should do it now, make a run for the door and slam it closed with her still inside. If I was fast enough, it could work, and I still had the element of surprise.

This time, I didn't bother to count.

My eyes popped open. I heard her quick intake of breath as I gained my feet and lunged for the door. It was so close! Another step, maybe two.

"Hendrik!" I shouted my brother's name to wake him, and I thought I heard a muffled groan. I was going to make it! The door was within reach.

Her bony hand clamped down on my shoulder, and I squirmed, trying to shake her off, when a sharp pain sent me to my knees. Liquid fire raced through my veins. I sucked in a breath, struggling to keep going, but her magic held me in place. The throb in my shoulder moved down my arm, and my eyes widened when my skin started to glow.

A burst of power expanded inside my body, shaking me to my core. The witch gasped and jerked her hand away. Stumbling through the cell door, she slammed the iron bars closed and removed the key.

She seethed on the other side, watching me tremble, unable to move. My arm had gone numb, but there was still a faint aura clinging to my skin and a humming in my veins. Her heartless gaze captured mine, and it took everything inside of me to hold that stare. A minute passed, then another. When the glow vanished, so did she. Spinning on her heel, she fled the room.

Air rushed from my lungs, and I fell forward onto my palms.

"Liana, are you all right?" Hendrik asked.

The witch had left the lantern, and I saw him sitting up in his cell rubbing the sleep from his eyes. I wanted to scream. I'd been so close! Crawling toward my meal, I flipped the tray of food, sending the bowl of gruel flying. I grabbed the wooden spoon, intending to throw it against the wall.

But something stopped me.

The numbness in my arm had faded, replaced with pins and needles, and the faint glow returned, growing stronger.

"Liana, what's happening?"

My voice trembled. "I don't know. The witch used magic on me. I can't explain it, but I think some of it's still inside me."

"Whoa." Hendrik's gaze landed on my fist where light bled from my fingers. I unfurled my hand, and the wooden spoon melted, morphing into another object.

A key.

Impossible.

The glow vanished, and so did the tingling sensation in my arm. I was left feeling drained and slightly dizzy. Whatever magic had transferred through me was gone, but it had given me exactly what I needed.

Scrambling across the floor on my knees, I slipped my hand between the bars and located the lock.

The key fit perfectly.

Hendrik's mouth hung open as I unlocked the cell and hurried to do the same to his. He climbed awkwardly to his feet, leaning heavily on one leg. I ducked under his shoulder to give him leverage as we hobbled toward the door.

He slowed our steps and whispered urgently near my ear, "If she catches us, I want you to run."

"What? No! I'm not leaving you here."

"You have to. With my leg the way it is, I'll only slow you down, and we'll both be trapped. I know it's hard, but you have to be brave. Promise me you'll run."

I drew in a deep breath, feeling the air as it shuddered inside my lungs. "I promise I'll come back for you."

"I know you will. Now, let's go."

The door creaked open, and we froze, listening for

the slightest sound. All I could hear was the rhythmic pounding of my heart. Slowly, we crept down the hallway. Each squeak of the floorboards made my breath catch.

Where was the witch?

The layout of the house was a fuzzy image in my mind. Its twisting turns and shadowed spaces left me worried we'd run into a dead end. Was it left at the end of the hallway or were we already heading in the wrong direction?

Placing my hand against the wall, I used it as a guide to navigate the dark. Heat rolled in waves down my back, making my thin shirt stick like a second skin. The potent scent of woodsmoke and incense clogged my throat, and I took shallow breaths to keep from coughing.

One hallway led to another before I felt the tiniest draft of cool air. In the next room, candles flickered, and I spotted a door. A narrow window—open a crack —let in a cool breeze.

"Wait," Hendrik whispered.

Something moved in the shadows. It all happened so fast as the witch appeared out of the dark, and Hendrik gave me a hard shove. I lost my balance and my grip on him. Falling to the floor, I looked up into the glowing eyes of the witch. But she wasn't watching me. Her bright gaze held Hendrik in place, and a scream bubbled in my throat when his eyes radiated the same flash of light.

"Run!" he shouted, unable to break free of the witch's spell. "Run and don't look back!"

My feet froze, refusing to move, until the witch lifted her hand toward me, fingers sparking with magic. I lunged for the door, throwing my weight against it. It shuddered open, and I tumbled through, landing shoulder-first in the dirt.

White light flooded my vision. I squinted to allow my eyes to adjust, taking in the dense trees, hard-packed earth, and the house towering over me like a monster ready to swallow me whole.

Fear and adrenaline kick-started my heart as I scrambled to my feet. *Run!* Hendrik's voice screamed inside my head, and I listened, rocks tearing through the thin soles of my shoes as I dove through the trees.

Heavy breaths whooshed in and out of my chest and a stitch burned in my side, but I ran faster, heedless of the thick branches that carved long scratches into my exposed skin. I didn't look back, certain if I did, I'd see the witch.

When a stump snagged my foot, I crashed to the ground, sliding through a bed of wet leaves. I rolled onto my back, trying to recapture my breath. The tree branches swirled overhead while I gulped air like a fish on dry land.

Slowly, my initial panic ebbed, and I sat up. The trees spread in every direction, each identical to the last. Somehow, I had to find help and go back for Hendrik, and if I wasn't careful, I'd end up hopelessly lost.

What if I couldn't find my way back to the house?

The realization clenched my stomach, and a sour taste filled my mouth. I squeezed my eyes shut against the sting of tears, but they dripped hot and wet onto the back of my hand.

When I opened my eyes again, my gaze landed on a peppermint candy that had fallen from my pocket. The pink swirls appeared overly bright against the dark leaves. Reaching into my pocket, I retrieved a handful of mints.

Choosing a direction, I weaved through the trees, dropping candies as I went. My supply dwindled, but I kept moving, scanning the forest for a way out.

It was ironic how time had meant so little while captive, but now, it meant everything, and I felt it slipping away. Already, the sun had dipped lower, and the dark I feared the most was coming.

Startled by the heavy thud of hooves, I ducked behind a tree. A short distance away, I spotted a rugged trail, and a rider came into view, followed by a small covered wagon.

Without thinking, I jumped in front of them. The men shouted, pulling back on their reins to avoid a collision. I fell on my backside, landing in the dirt as the man on the horse dismounted.

"Thomas, why have we stopped?" A woman peeked through the canvas-topped wagon. She gasped when she saw me.

Thomas knelt at my side, his gaze roaming over my knotted hair and mud-caked hands. "Where did you come from?" he asked. "We're miles outside the kingdom."

The words were thick on my tongue, but I forced them out in a jumble of scattered thoughts. "My brother. I have to go back for Hendrik. The witch has him."

"Witch?" A look passed between the two men.

Climbing from the wagon, the woman crouched beside Thomas. "What's your name, dear?"

"Liana. Please, I can take you there, but we have to hurry." I unfurled my hand, showing them the few remaining candies in my palm. "I left a trail."

Thomas stood and nodded toward the man driving the wagon. They each mounted a horse, and Thomas addressed the woman.

"Wait here with the girl, Sarah. We'll see if we can find anyone."

I watched helplessly as they disappeared into the trees. The woman nudged me toward the wagon and offered me a drink of water. I drank greedily from the canteen, nearly choking on the cool liquid.

"Go easy," Sarah murmured, watching me with concern.

I handed her back the canteen, and she opened the canvas flap on the wagon, gesturing for me to climb inside. I couldn't do it. The gaping hole looked like the mouth of a monster. My whole body trembled as I backed away from the wagon.

Sarah held up her hand and lowered the flap. "It's okay—we can wait outside. Why don't you tell me a little more about yourself?"

Time passed slowly as the shadows deepened and evening bled into night. I shivered under a blanket while Sarah gently probed me with more questions. The last of the candies melted in my hand, making my palm sticky, and the scent of mint filled my nose.

All around us, night sounds battered my ears. The wind flapped the awning, and an owl hooted somewhere high above. And then finally, I heard the horses as they returned to the trail.

My heart cracked against my rib cage as Sarah stood and gestured for me to stay seated. She stepped away from the wagon and lowered her voice.

"Did you find him?"

An eerie silence descended, and then Thomas's grave tone filled the void.

"We found a house in a small clearing." His voice dropped to a low whisper. "It was empty, but someone had been there recently. The embers in the hearth were still warm."

"But the girl—"

"We were too late, Sarah. She's the only one who escaped."

Chapter 2

Bowen

Six years later...

"He's a beast! A man with a wicked temper who'd rather cut you than look at you. Why else would he collect all these weapons? The catacombs beneath this manor must be filled with his prey." The merchant waved his arm through the air, indicating the expansive display of knives and broadswords hanging from the wall.

"Maybe so, Charles, but he pays well." The other merchant, the one named Thomas, leaned forward to examine a painting. His eyes widened at the macabre scene.

I slid into the shadows on the other side of the wall. Could he see me? Impossible. It was unlikely Thomas had noticed the two peepholes drilled into the tree line. However, when I peered through the holes again, I studied the man to be sure.

Charles scoffed. "What use is a fortune if we end up chained in the basement, subject to his torture devices? His scars alone could send a man screaming.

Have you seen his face?"

My fingers pressed reflexively over the scar in question. It bisected my left eye and carved a path under my chin to the collarbone. More scars disappeared beneath the neckline of my shirt.

I sneered. What did that man know about torture? Had he ever watched the razor's edge of a blade descend against his skin? Feel its teeth as it left its mark, knowing even though it wouldn't cause death, it would leave a different kind of permanence—one that inspired fear?

No. That man knew nothing.

I pulled a hidden lever on the wall, and the platform spun on silent tracks. The merchants were too engrossed in their conversation to notice I'd joined them in the room. I crossed my forearms over my chest and waited.

Thomas shrugged. "I haven't seen his face, but it doesn't matter. We're here to deliver the blade, not make friends."

"With his reputation, I doubt Bowen MacKenzie has any friends." Charles picked up a cast-iron cannonball and weighed it in his palm. He held it up to show Thomas and gave a strangled cry when he spotted me. The cannonball slipped from his hand and cracked against the floor before rolling underneath my desk. He gulped. "How long has he been standing there?"

"Long enough," I muttered.

Charles blanched and swayed on his feet. "We meant no offense."

"Then I must have misheard you." Crossing to my desk, I lowered myself into the chair. It creaked beneath my large frame. Steepling my fingers together, I rested my elbows on the surface and glared.

Perfected over the years, my glare accentuated my scars and sent even the hardiest men to their knees. Charles was no exception. His left knee buckled, but he caught himself before he hit the floor.

"Did you bring it?" I asked, shifting my attention to Thomas.

Thomas nodded. The hardier of the two, he only swallowed and tugged the collar of his shirt away from his neck. He didn't break my gaze, which surprised me. Most people were reluctant to look me in the eye. Many preferred to direct their conversation at the floor.

"We brought the blade and have done what you asked. Anyone looking for the weapon will be able to track it back to you."

"Good," I growled.

A tense silence followed in which both merchants apparently forgot their purpose. Their gazes dropped to their feet. *Typical.* I rapped my knuckles on the desk.

"I don't have all day. The blade. Now."

Thomas stumbled forward, and in his haste, the case thumped heavily onto the desk. He flinched at the sound and mumbled an apology. Charles nearly fainted—again.

I grinned, flashing my teeth. Trouble was, my grin didn't have a soothing effect. The opposite in fact. Charles paled and stepped backward, bumping into a display case. The glass door rattled but thankfully didn't shatter. If it did, I'd probably have an unconscious man lying on my pristine rug.

This was getting old and far too predictable.

Expelling an irritated breath, I lifted the lid on the case and ignored the clumsy twosome. Nestled against a red velvet liner was the Grimm's blade. My predatory grin softened into a contented smirk. Finally, the revenge I sought was at hand.

Gently, I removed the dagger and examined it in the light. The craftsmanship was incredible. Colorful jewels of varying sizes encrusted the hilt, and the tip of the blade glinted, its sharpness seeming to mock other blades. It was safe to say I'd never seen an equal. But what truly made the dagger special was its infusion of magic, making it not only deadly to humans but certain supernatural creatures as well.

"Who's the craftsman?" I asked with an awed whisper.

When neither merchant answered, I fixed a vicious glare on Charles. He coughed into his hand.

"The craftsman?" I demanded.

"More like crafts...woman, sir," Charles stammered. "His daughter Liana Archer forged the weapon. It's some of her finest work."

Thomas's jaw tightened, and he frowned at his business partner's revelation. "Enough, Charles."

"Your daughter?" My brow creased. It was surprising but made perfect sense. There was a delicate attention to detail and an almost enchanting curve in the steel. Her skill was undeniable. The blade sucked you in like a siren's sweet voice, begging for the chance to slide between your ribs. *It won't hurt a bit,* it promised.

I placed the blade back into the box and opened my desk drawer. For the past few years, I'd searched for someone with the ability to create mystical weapons. Few had the gift, and those who did remained hidden, selling their wares anonymously. It wasn't a mystery why Thomas wanted to keep his daughter's abilities a secret.

To many, my collection appeared to be a sickness, but to me, it was a cure. I thrived on the artistry it took to create an object as beautiful as it was deadly, and there was one weapon I wanted above all others. I had spent nights hunched over my worktable scratching pen across parchment, trying to recapture the design I'd only seen once before.

I placed a scroll on the desk. "Will she take a commission?" My heart raced while I waited for an answer. Hope bloomed inside my chest, a rare emotion not often found there.

"No."

His refusal was curt and final. The rage must have shown on my face, because Charles made a noise in the back of his throat and looked pleadingly at Thomas to reconsider.

My brow arched. "No?"

"I'm afraid not, sir. I won't ask it of her."

"Why not?" I dared Thomas to reveal his reason even though I knew why. The answer was in his eyes:

He didn't want a man like me anywhere near his daughter. My presence might sully her, dim her talent, and make her fearful.

Normally, I found pleasure in the ability to elicit fear. It was intoxicating and addictive. It handed me control where control had been stripped from me in the past. But this time, denial formed on my lips, and an ache materialized in my chest where hope had been. I needed to meet the woman who wielded such remarkable talent. It was a gut feeling; a soul-deep understanding she would appreciate how something as ugly as a tool of death could still be beautiful to look at.

"No" wasn't an option.

"I'll pay you double."

Thomas shook his head.

"Triple."

Charles sucked in a breath, and this time, his right knee buckled.

"I'm sorry, but I must decline." He bowed then cleared his throat. "We've completed our transaction and would be grateful if you allowed us to leave with our payment."

Leaning back in my chair, I crossed my arms over my chest and made him wait before responding. "I can see you won't be persuaded."

"I will not."

"Very well. You will be paid on your way out. Though, I insist you stay long enough for my cook to prepare a basket of food for your journey home."

"That would be most generous of you, sir!" Charles

beamed, grateful the negotiations had ended and I hadn't led them both into my basement at knifepoint.

Thomas looked wary but nodded his consent. The two merchants backed out of the room, and I returned my gaze to the Grimm's blade. I wasn't the only one searching for the mystical weapon; I was just the one who'd gotten to it first.

Pride and anticipation flowed through my veins, though it wasn't as satisfying as I imagined. There was nothing stronger than getting revenge on those responsible for ruining my life, so why did the thought of a mysterious woman give me pause? My fingers drummed the desktop as an idea formed.

Did I dare?

A sharp rap on the door claimed my focus, and I spotted my friend Gavin leaning in through the doorway.

"The merchant's carriage is being prepared. They should be on their way soon."

My reckless thought returned, taking hold with gripping force. I'd have to act quickly.

Motioning Gavin closer, I rose from my chair and rested my fists on the desktop. "They look like fine men, don't they? Certainly not the type to steal."

Gavin's brow furrowed, but then a slow smile spread across his face. "I'd say not, Bowen."

My lips flattened. "Unfortunately, I have placed my trust in the wrong people before."

"You have."

I walked toward a display cabinet, searching for just the right piece. *There.* I opened the glass door and removed a diamond-encrusted scepter. On the outside, the scepter appeared purely ornamental, but inside, it hid a hollow shaft where a capsule of poison resided. But I didn't plan on poisoning anyone. I had a different crime in mind.

"This looks expensive, doesn't it?"

"It's probably worth more than my family home." Gavin's grin widened. He was enjoying our little game.

"What do you think would happen if it wound up inside the merchants' carriage?"

Gavin slapped a hand to his chest in mock horror. "Well, they'd likely get away with it."

I rubbed the scar along my jawline with my thumb and debated whether this distraction was worth the risk. Could I have my revenge and my commission? Thomas's strong refusal echoed in my mind. I should leave the girl alone. She'd already done enough by crafting the blade that would help exact my revenge.

But they had piqued my interest. There was no going back.

"Someone should alert the authorities then." I tossed the scepter to Gavin and matched his wicked grin. "I've been robbed."

"I'll make sure they're alerted right away. After I hide this in the merchants' carriage." He winked.

"Let the authorities know I intend to press charges unless we can strike some sort of deal. Possibly an exchange of services?"

"I'm sure everyone involved will be amenable to your offer."

I laughed, the action pulling my scars tight. I

highly doubted that. It would have been so much easier if Thomas hadn't said no. He'd given me no choice.

After Gavin left to do my bidding, I wandered toward the window overlooking the grounds. The merchants' carriage was still parked on the driveway. I placed my fingers against the glass, feeling the icy sting from the chilly morning. Frost tipped the overgrown lawn, the weeds thinning near the rocky cliffs leading down to the ocean's surf.

If I felt the tiniest prick of guilt, I smothered it. I'd have my revenge, and I'd have my commission. I'd have it all. No one would ever deny me again.

The merchants came into view, laughing and slapping each other on the backs from their windfall. I'd paid them a fortune. Too bad where they were headed, they wouldn't be able to spend it. After they were settled inside the carriage, it jolted forward, disappearing down the driveway, the passengers oblivious to their stolen cargo and the trap I'd set.

Chapter 3

Liana

"Tell us a story!"

I thrust the length of steel into the smoldering coals and glanced down at the set of six-year-old twins. Bridget and Benjamin fidgeted on the balls of their feet, their eyes wide with expectation.

"A story? I told you one last night before bed." Pushing a loose strand of hair out of my eyes, I stepped away from the heated forge.

Bridget frowned, her fairylike features scrunching in displeasure. "But you always leave off the ending."

My lips flattened, and I made a disgusted sound in the back of my throat. *Because nothing good ever comes from an ending.*

Benjamin crossed his short arms. "We're not scared, Liana. We're almost seven!"

I chuckled and reached for the top of Benjamin's head, tousling the soft strands. "Hmm...you're right. You are getting older. I thought I saw some gray hairs in here the other day."

"We're serious." Bridget mimicked her brother's

stubborn pose, and I sighed. The two of them were little terrors, but I couldn't say no whenever they stuck together. They reminded me too much of Hendrik and myself.

"All right, fine. But you asked for it." I waggled my finger and deepened my voice, taking on the throaty cackle of the villain. "After the prince and the princess slayed the witch, they rode off into the sunset. And they all lived...until one day, the witch returned to lure—"

"Liana Archer!" Sarah hissed from the doorway. She stepped into the room and clapped her hands. "That's enough storytime for today, you two. Run into the house and wash up for dinner."

The twins groaned as they filed out of the workshop, while I cast Sarah a glare for ruining my story.

"Why did you stop me? They should know the truth. Love doesn't conquer all, and sometimes, the ones you love disappear and it's all your fault. Happily ever after doesn't exist, and anyone telling them differently is selling them something." Crossing to my workbench, I picked up my latest creation and tightened my grip around the hilt. Pointing the tip, I stepped into a lunge. "'Fend for yourself,' is what I always say. And never assume the witch is dead. They always come back."

Sarah's shoulders slumped in defeat, and she sat heavily in a chair beside my workbench. "What happened wasn't your fault."

I ignored her reply because I'd heard it all before. I

could recite the rest of her speech in my sleep. Sarah and Thomas had been trying to convince me of it from the moment they took me in after that fateful day. The speech always ended with, "Your brother would have been so proud to see the woman you are today."

Ugh, I hated that part. Who cared about how someone might have felt? For all I knew, Hendrik resented me for not finding him in time. Here I was, with my new family and comfortable home. It wasn't fair. Where was his rescuer on a white horse?

Besides, it was my fault. Not only was I too late, but the witch had kidnapped us because of me. It wasn't until after I'd settled in with the Archers I discovered the extent of my power. I had the ability to transfer magic, taking it from one place and putting it into another, just like I did when I absorbed the witch's magic and used it to create a key. The witch had known about my ability—it was what she'd whispered while leaning over me before I tried to escape.

"Liana, I wish you would—"

Sarah's plea was interrupted when the door to the workshop burst open and our maid, Lucy, rushed inside. She twisted her ruffled cap and choked back tears.

"Mrs. Archer, I have terrible news."

Sarah stood, leaning heavily against the chair. Even the simple act of standing caused the breath to wheeze in her throat. She was getting worse. The illness was spreading faster than we imagined.

"What is it, Lucy?"

The maid's lips trembled. "It's Mr. Archer. He and

Mr. Edwin are being held in the royal prison. They're accused of stealing a jeweled scepter from Lord MacKenzie."

"That's absurd!" I sputtered, looking to Sarah to make sure the news hadn't sent her into one of her coughing spells.

"They were caught with the scepter in their carriage. Lord MacKenzie is pressing charges."

"Is there anything we can do?" Sarah asked, sinking back into the chair. Her face had taken on an ashen appearance, and she placed a hand against the base of her throat.

Lucy lifted her shoulders in a helpless shrug. "Their sentencing is tomorrow unless a family member can plead their case, but you aren't well enough to travel across the channel."

"I'll go," I said, my stomach already churning with nerves at the thought of leaving the village.

"You can't go, Liana. You know how you get. What if you have one of your attacks?"

"I said I'm going." There was steel in my tone, but not in my spine. Sarah had good reason to worry. I'd spent the past six years hiding in our remote village. I was probably the only woman my age afraid of the dark, and I was terrified of enclosed spaces. I needed the wide-open fields of our village where even the dark felt familiar and safe.

"Everything will be fine. I'll go directly to the authorities. This will all be straightened out tomorrow, and the three of us will return safe and sound." My muscles tightened, and those first terrifying seconds of paralysis crept through my body. Going back to the kingdom where everything had started made me want to lock the door to my workshop and hide in the hayloft.

I'd failed Hendrik all those years ago, and now, thanks to my crippling anxiety, I might fail Thomas too. The man who'd adopted me and tried valiantly to fix what was broken inside. But it couldn't be fixed, only faced, and I refused to let him spend the rest of his life in prison for something he didn't do.

There wasn't any other choice. I was getting Thomas out of prison, one way or another.

***

A sheen of cold sea mist coated my skin as I stared at the approaching coastline. My grip tightened around the satchel pressed to my hip, and I braced my legs against the dip and sway of the ship's motion.

I'd spent hours crossing the channel above deck, taking in the fresh, salty air and trying to come up with a plan. The meager amount of coins in my satchel weren't likely to set Thomas or Mr. Edwin free, and the gulls overhead seemed to swoop and cry their agreement as if they could read my mind.

I knew a little about the man who'd accused Thomas of theft. Mostly anecdotes from stories floating around our village. His daring adventures were fodder for the gossips, but the later stories made him sound more like a villain from a fairy tale than an actual person. Bowen MacKenzie was a treasure hunter who'd found fame and fortune discovering some of the kingdom's most prized artifacts until his last expedition ended in disaster. Now, the dashing adventurer was a disfigured recluse who'd gained the nickname "Bowen the Beast."

I heaved a sigh and grumbled under my breath, "Just my luck. Thomas couldn't have been accused by the local baker, could he? Figures it would be by a man with an ominous nickname."

The ship docked before I was ready, and I followed the other passengers down the narrow gangway. With my feet firmly planted on solid ground, I scanned the crowd swarming the harbor.

"Which way to the agency?" I asked a sailor unloading luggage, but he shrugged and walked off with a crate balanced on his shoulder.

A hysterical laugh bubbled in my throat. I swiped my sleeve across my brow. This was crazy! I didn't know where I was going or even what I planned to say when I got there.

Thomas's steady voice echoed in my ears, and I drew in a deep breath. *Don't think of everything you have to do, only the task in front of you.* He'd instilled that saying into me whenever a problem seemed too overwhelming, and this seemed like a good time to put his advice to use. First, I needed to find the agency. I'd worry about the rest later.

Leaving the docks, I walked down an alley that led to the main thoroughfare. Carriages rumbled past, weaving recklessly between shouting pedestrians. Tall buildings of wood and stone flanked both sides of the road, and the air was cleaner than the fish and sweat-infused atmosphere of the wharf.

I stood on the edge of the street, cursing my height while trying to see over the tops of men double my size. Someone jostled me from behind, and I stumbled into the roadway, landing hard on my palms.

Dirt and rocks embedded themselves into my skin as a cloud of dust blurred my vision. I cursed, brushing my stinging palms against my skirt. A sound thundered in my ears, rising above the general chaos in the street. I looked up to see giant hooves crushing gravel into the cobblestones, headed straight for me.

"Get out of the way, lady!" the carriage driver snarled, jerking on the reins.

Snarling back, I scrambled to my feet. The driver didn't wait for me to leave the roadway. He maneuvered around me, the carriage wheels nearly taking off my toes.

Anger churned inside my stomach. I hadn't been in the kingdom five minutes and I'd already wound up in the dirt. Gritting my teeth, I sidestepped another rolling pedestrian killer and reached beneath my cloak to wrap my fingers around the hilt of my favorite dagger.

Knowing I had the familiar weapon so close eased some of my tension. After escaping the witch, I vowed never to allow myself to be caught defenseless again, and it was an element of control I found reassuring.

Further down the lane, I finally located the spike-tipped gates that surrounded the royal agency. The kingdom's seal glittered in the sunshine above the doorway, and long woven banners fluttered lazily in the breeze. I crossed the street, pausing as another carriage rolled past. This one was different from the others. The vehicle was sleek and black, with thick coverings over the windows giving privacy to the occupants inside. It rumbled to a stop outside the agency gates, and the sea of people parted, giving it a wide berth.

The number of onlookers grew. They whispered behind their hands, some outright gawking at the parked carriage. Even though their stares were brazen, a rising trepidation emanated from the crowd; a nervousness that reminded me of when the fair came to our village and the revelers approached the creature exhibits with giddy fascination mixed with a healthy dose of fear. I waited for the passenger to exit, wondering who could have caused the disturbance.

The door opened, and a man dressed fully in black emerged from the vehicle. He paid no attention to the gaping audience or the fact they stumbled back, increasing their distance, as he pushed through the iron gate. His formidable frame bounded up the stone steps.

"That's him!" someone beside me gasped. "That's Bowen the Beast."

I craned my neck, watching his progress until he disappeared behind the heavy-looking wooden door. The noise from the crowd dimmed, turning into a buzzing nuisance.

So that was Bowen MacKenzie?

His height alone should have sent me scurrying back to the ship, but there was something captivating about him that kept me rooted in place. Maybe it was the way he seemed to manipulate the crowd, as if a single gesture from his powerful arms would send them scattering into the wind. He plowed through with intent and an air of authority I found enthralling.

As the crowd thinned, I forced myself to take the first few steps up the agency staircase. I peered at the engraved seal above the door and squared my shoulders.

Straightening to my full five foot three inches, I reviewed my newly formed plan: Storm the agency, demand my father's release, and—if I could help it—try not to end up in a cell next to him for threatening them all with the blade at my hip.

Chapter 4

Liana

The agency clerk put down her pen and smiled politely as I approached her desk. It was a smile born from years of dealing with the public, laced with an underlying impatience that did little to calm my nerves.

"Can I help you, Miss?"

I smoothed damp palms down the front of my cloak and tried not to fidget. "Yes, my name is Liana Archer. I'm here to plead my father's case. He's been arrested, and I'm certain there's been a terrible mistake."

The woman angled her brow, deepening the fine lines around her eyes. Her half-smile suggested she'd heard it all before. "A mistake, hmm? You said your last name was Archer?" She glanced at her ledger and ran a wrinkled finger down the list of names. "I'm assuming your father is Thomas Archer? The man caught stealing from Bowen MacKenzie."

My teeth clenched. "He didn't steal anything."

She pursed her lips and folded her hands together. "Because it was a mistake?"

"Yes!"

"How original," she said dryly. "Have a seat, please. I'll inform Detective Chambers you're here." She pointed toward a line of rigid chairs set against a dark-paneled wall. The first few chairs were occupied, so I walked to the far end and settled in to wait.

As the minutes ticked by, I drew in a slow breath. Any lingering nerves were replaced with a swell of irritation. Thomas was an honest man. He'd never stolen anything in his life, and neither had his business partner Charles Edwin. There had to be a way to prove their innocence. Though, given the skepticism of the clerk, it appeared providing character references wouldn't be much help.

Minutes stretched into a half-hour as I waited for the detective. The chairs beside me emptied and refilled. My irritation reached a tipping point, and I launched from my seat to pace the room. On my third lap, a bulletin board caught my attention.

The board was covered with sheets of parchment detailing lost items, suspicious circumstances, and a series of wanted posters. But what drew my eye was the drawing of a teenage boy. His unsmiling face and gaunt cheekbones sent a shiver of foreboding down my spine. I tried to shake it. Adults and children vanished all the time in a kingdom as large as this. So many succumbed to the hardships of living on the street or were runaways. Most had no one to report them missing.

There was no sign the boy had been taken, yet his features morphed into a familiar face that pleaded with me to come back for him. The room narrowed, the walls closing in. Waves of dry heat flamed my skin, and the phantom scent of mint filled my nose. Darkness crept into the corners of my vision as Hendrik's urgent cry echoed in my ears.

Make it stop!

I spun and staggered away from the board, only to collide with an immovable object. Ironlike hands clamped over my shoulders, steadying me from the force of the impact. I tilted my head back, blinking away the swirling darkness.

My gaze connected with a pair of copper-colored eyes flecked with gold. The man had thick strands of dark hair that framed a hawkish nose and chiseled cheekbones. His mouth was firm, deepening into a scowl the longer I stared. And I did stare, shocked to find the panicked flight that possessed my body had faded, and even though his grip held me in place, there was a subtleness making me believe I wasn't truly trapped. Given the slightest resistance, his hands would drop away, allowing me to escape.

What a strange feeling, to be imprisoned and free at the same time.

It was then I observed the scars. A jagged slash peeked from beneath the strands of hair, running the length of his jaw. It marred the flesh, a juxtaposition to the skin that was so flawless on the other side. Smaller scars crisscrossed the larger one, vanishing beneath the collar of his coat. His fingers stiffened around my shoulders when he realized where my gaze had stalled.

I brought my focus back to his eyes, and he flinched. His arms dropped to his sides, but the heavy sensation of his hands still lingered in the same way the ghost of mint had captured my senses.

"You're here." His voice was deep like the low rumble of thunder before a rainstorm.

I frowned and broke his gaze, stepping out of the oddly soothing bubble I'd found myself in. I recognized him as Bowen MacKenzie, the man who'd charged through the crowd earlier and had accused my father of theft. But he spoke as if he knew me, unsurprised Thomas Archer's daughter stood before him. Almost as if he knew I'd come.

Wariness made me take another step back. *Never trust a stranger no matter what your gut tells you.* Somehow, I had to convince this man to release my father, and I couldn't let a few tantalizing moments sway me from my purpose.

"Lord MacKenzie, we weren't finished with our discussion." Another man stepped into view. He was the same height as Bowen, with similar broad shoulders, but this man was more refined and had the classically handsome features women usually swooned over.

Assuming the man in front of me was my father's accuser, that meant the newcomer was likely the detective handling the case. I angled my body away from Bowen and addressed the detective, but I could still feel the weight of his gaze against my back. I may have dismissed him, but he hadn't dismissed me.

"Detective Chambers? My name is Liana Archer,

and I'm here to negotiate the release of my father and his business partner. I understand they were arrested for theft." I darted a glance at Bowen, cursing the action when our gazes locked and heat climbed to my cheeks. Clearing my throat, I continued. "Neither my father nor Mr. Edwin are thieves. It's obvious to me there's been a misunderstanding. I insist you release them while we work through this situation."

"You insist?" Bowen's mouth curved into a smirk. "They were caught with a priceless item from my collection inside their carriage. How do you explain it got there, Miss Archer?"

My mouth opened to answer, but nothing came out. The heat from my cheeks sank into my belly from the way he drew out the syllables of my name. It was like warm honey sliding down a knife.

I scrounged around for a reply that would knock some of the smug confidence off his face and give me a fighting chance.

Angling my head back to meet his gaze, I said, "I suspect someone planted it."

Bowen tensed. Surprise flashed across his features before his eyes narrowed in challenge. "Are you accusing me, Miss Archer? Be careful. Many have lived to regret such an act."

"Is that a threat?" My hands landed on my hips.

Detective Chambers stepped between us. "Miss Archer, if you would follow me into my office, we can discuss your father's case further. Under normal circumstances, we would proceed with sentencing, but after a conversation with Lord MacKenzie, he's willing to drop the charges if reparations are made."

The detective gestured down the hall, but I refused to move from my spot. They weren't taking me to some isolated room for more intimidation. I should have seen this coming. Justice wasn't going to be served or even considered. I'd have to pay our way out of this situation, and depending on how much Bowen wanted, I might need to pawn my lucky blade. I cringed at the thought. A pawn shop wouldn't give me what it was worth. They never did.

"How much does he want?" Disgust dripped from my tone.

"I have no use for your money, Miss Archer." Bowen didn't move either, and the detective rubbed the bridge of his nose in frustration, realizing our negotiation was going to take place in the lobby.

Bowen folded his arms over his chest and towered over me. "They stole a weapon from me, and it's a weapon I want in return."

I mimicked his pose and smiled sweetly. "I'm sure Detective Chambers will gladly return the weapon found in the carriage. You've lost nothing, sir."

He stalked closer, daring me to retreat. "I've already lost a great deal. Time, money…" He took another step as he muttered the last word under his breath. It sounded like "sanity," but I couldn't be sure. His gaze raked from the top of my head to my toes. "I hear you're a skilled weaponsmith, and I'm also aware of your unique abilities regarding magic. Are you willing to bargain for your father's release? Are you willing to take his place?"

He knows about my gift? My mind raced, but I was less worried about his knowledge of my skill and more by his question. A flash of panic rose inside my chest, and I choked on my reply.

"You mean, take his place in prison?"

Bowen chuckled. "No, Miss Archer, though some would say living with me is worse than prison. You'll have to tell me if they're right."

The crook of his lips sent my temper flaring. "Live with you? What kind of bargain is this?" I jabbed my finger into his chest, almost wishing it were my dagger instead. He wouldn't think he could walk all over me then.

"Miss Archer," Detective Chambers said, trying to diffuse the situation. Everyone in the waiting room had stopped to stare, and the clerk leaned forward over her desk in rapt interest. "What Lord MacKenzie is suggesting—poorly, I might add—is a term of indentured servitude." His gaze darkened on Bowen, and there was censure in his tone. "The terms state you'll live at MacKenzie Manor until you've completed a commissioned weapon for his collection. It's unorthodox, but not unheard of. If you accept the terms, you'll be considered an employee, nothing more. Isn't that right, MacKenzie?"

"Correct, Detective. Miss Archer will be free to go when she's finished with her work."

I leaned in, anger making me bold. My voice dropped to a whisper. "And what makes you think I won't create the weapon and use it against you?"

To my frustration, a gleam of admiration appeared

in his eyes. "A few have tried, Miss Archer, evidenced by the scars on my skin. But it will take more than that to kill me." He lowered his head, warm breath skating over my ear. "Are you willing to give it a go?"

Trapped.

I'd marveled earlier at how he hadn't made me feel that way, but the snare had tightened, and now I was truly caught. Sure, I could turn him down and return home without Thomas, but I couldn't do that to Sarah. To either of them. After everything they'd done for me, this sacrifice paled in comparison.

"You'll release my father and Mr. Edwin?"

Bowen nodded. "As you keep insisting."

A shaky feeling of alarm rushed through my body, and I tried to tamp it down, resigning myself to the bargain. Bowen must have sensed my surrender because he grinned—an act that twisted his scars. A grin like his was meant to intimidate. He knew the effect it had, but he didn't know I'd seen worse and had spent the past few years hardening my defenses.

But defenses weren't only made of wood and steel. Sometimes, they hid in the way we responded to threats. Better to act accordingly and let him think he'd won.

His grin widened, and I pretended to flinch beneath it, only to watch his smile dim. Something like regret flashed across his features, and he lifted his hand as if he meant to brush away the fear he'd incited.

He had a vulnerability. The realization popped into my head without warning. He'd shown the tiniest crack in an armor he thought impenetrable. I could exploit that. Maybe use it to my advantage. Either way, I planned to see this through.

I held out my hand. "Fine, Lord MacKenzie. You have a deal."

Chapter 5

Bowen

My hand closed over hers to seal the agreement. It was small and fine-boned. However, there were calluses where smooth skin should be—proof of her skilled profession. There was even a thin scar at the base of her thumb, and I wondered how she'd received it.

She wore a floor-length leather cloak tied underneath her chin and a navy blue dress laced over a darker-hued bodice. Long blonde hair hung in silken waves down her back, and glossy strands curled over her shoulders. There was a jittery nervousness about her that switched into fierceness in an instant. A strange mixture of emotions in a woman who barely reached my shoulders.

My grip tightened around her fingers. Maybe if she hadn't come, I could have let this entire thing go. I had more than enough problems without adding one of my own making. But it was too late. She was here, and the trap had been set.

The victory tasted sweet. So sweet I wasn't able to control the gruesome smile that spread across my lips.

The same smile that caused Charles Edwin to nearly collapse in fear. A smile I usually wielded as a weapon. But that was the thing about weapons: they drew blood no matter the target, and when Liana shrank beneath mine, I regretted the act.

Yet an odd thing happened next. Her eyes flicked up for the barest of seconds, as if she were calculating my reaction, and I wondered if my smile had drawn blood at all, or if maybe she was wielding a weapon of her own.

A scoff burst from my throat. This slip of a woman had threatened to forge a weapon and use it against me. It was unbelievable. There hadn't been fear in her eyes then. Loathing more than anything, but also a deep well of stubbornness. So unlike everyone else. She wasn't typical at all, and if I had any sense, I'd watch my back.

"I'd like to see my father before we go, if that's possible," she said, removing her hand from mine and turning her attention to Detective Chambers.

The detective nodded. "He's currently at the royal prison, and it might be a few hours before we can get him processed and brought over."

"That's too long to wait. I have a schedule to keep." The last thing I needed was for Thomas Archer to talk her out of the deal or plant suspicions in her head that I set him up. Besides, my skin felt tight from being in town for too long. The knowing stares and staged whispers were already taking their toll.

She tossed me an irritated snarl. "Do you have time for me to write him a note? He'll show up on your manor's doorstep if I don't."

The clerk tore a sheet from her ledger and held out her pen. "You can use this if you'd like."

Liana didn't wait for my answer and moved toward the desk to write her letter. The clerk leaned back in her chair and continued to watch the scene unfold in amusement. It seemed we were her entertainment for the day.

Long minutes passed in which Liana chewed the corner of her lip, trying to come up with the right words. My patience ebbed, and when she finally put down the pen and folded the note in half, I expelled an irritated sigh.

"Finished, or have you changed your mind and reneged on our deal?"

She handed the letter to Detective Chambers and stalked toward me. The soles of her shoes clicked heavily against the floor. "I agreed to your terms. You'll have your commission, and then you'll set me free. It's a small price to pay to save my father from a life sentence." Brushing past me, she swept down the short corridor toward the exit.

Yeah, I should definitely watch my back.

Detective Chambers pushed away from the clerk's desk and sauntered toward me. A smirk played around the corners of his mouth. He crossed his arms, his features sobering as he addressed me.

"One of my men will be by to check on Miss Archer's situation. I expect to find her a satisfied employee, or I'll have to reassess this deal. You aren't above the law, MacKenzie, no matter how many gold coins line your pockets."

My jaw clenched. "Miss Archer will be well taken care of and returned as soon as she completes her commission. You have my word, Detective."

"See that she is."

I stifled a retort, eager to be on my way.

Outside, the air had chilled and the morning sunshine had disappeared as midday ushered in ominous gray clouds. Liana stood on the top step staring intently at my carriage. She twisted her fingers nervously in the folds of her cloak, oblivious to my looming presence.

"Carriages don't bite," I grumbled, hurrying past her down the steps. The iron gate screeched as I thrust it open, and my driver bowed as he held the carriage door. I climbed up the step and slid along the cushioned seat, waiting for her to follow.

She didn't.

My boot rapped against the floor for a full minute, the nervous energy sliding up my bones until I clenched my fists. Hesitantly, Liana approached the carriage. Poking her head inside, she surveyed the tight, shadowed space. Her nose scrunched as if she found my luxury vehicle distasteful.

"What's the problem?"

She winced at my tone. "May I ride up top with the driver?"

"No." I swung forward and grasped her arm, hauling her inside the carriage.

The moment the door closed, the vehicle rumbled into motion, and she lost her balance, falling awkwardly into my lap. Liana shrieked, tangled in her cloak and mass of long hair. Thrashing her arms, she scuttled into the seat across from me. She whipped her hair out of her eyes and gulped in a lungful of air. Her fingers gripped the seat cushion as if it were a floating ship's plank and the only thing keeping her from sinking into the deep.

Stark shadows created by the weak glow of the lantern hanging from the ceiling played over her features, but they couldn't hide her pinched expression or the bluish tint expanding across her cheeks. I realized with a jolt she hadn't let out her last breath.

"Relax," I snapped. And then, with a softer growl, "Breathe."

Her glassy eyes found mine, and air whooshed past her lips only to be sucked back in on a rapid inhale. She was panicked. Beads of sweat formed on her brow, and when the carriage hit a rut, making the lantern swing, her eyes snapped shut.

Concern washed away my irritation. I came off the seat and knelt in front of her. This wasn't a normal reaction to driving down the street, and I was loath to pin it on any fear of traveling with me. My hands hovered uselessly in the air, afraid my touch would send her leaping from the moving carriage.

Liana's eyes remained closed as she fumbled for her something at her waist. The flash of steel rocked me back on my heels when she unsheathed a dagger. I tensed, ready for her to lodge it deep into my chest. Now, I was the one holding my breath.

Who knew it wasn't my back I needed to watch, but my front?

"Liana," I mumbled her name, voice wary.

"I'm fine. I just don't like enclosed spaces," she whispered, pressing the blade flat against her chest, embracing it. Her features relaxed, and even when the carriage rocked a second time, the blade seemed to have a soothing effect.

Reluctantly, I moved back to my seat, thankful she hadn't skewered me but also oddly shaken. She clung to the blade like a child clutching their favorite toy, finding security in its presence.

Breathing easier, she lowered the dagger and opened her eyes. The ride evened out as we left town and turned down the deserted road that led to the manor. With the crowds and onlookers gone, I pulled back the heavy draperies covering the windows. She seemed to relax further, though she maintained a tight grip around the dagger's hilt.

I cleared my throat, keeping a distrustful eye on her weapon. "Thank you for not stabbing the upholstery. It's quite difficult to replace."

Something resembling a smile flickered across her features, and I felt a tiny surge of relief. She shifted closer to the window, turning her face up like a flower seeking the sun.

We traveled for a distance in silence. The only sounds were the clack of the carriage wheels and the steady beat of the horses' hooves.

I ran my thumb absently over a scar at the base of my collarbone. What to talk about? There really wasn't much of an icebreaker after you extorted services from someone and they had a panic attack inside a moving carriage. It didn't seem appropriate to pry into her private life, yet asking about the weather didn't seem appropriate either.

I tried it anyway—the weather, not her secrets.

"It seems as if it might snow soon. The clouds are..."—I leaned forward and glanced out the window—"ominous."

She didn't react or give any sign my trivial conversation starter had interested her. Who could blame her? *The clouds are ominous.* My insides shriveled. This sort of thing—charming women and claiming their interest—used to be easy for me. It had always come as naturally as breathing. A devastating smile, a devilish arch of my brow, and plenty of daring stories from my treasure-hunting days had them hanging off every word.

But that was before. Now, every expression felt tainted, and there were no more bold adventures.

Better to stick to the business at hand.

"I'll show you the plans I've made for your commission after you've had some time to get settled. The sooner you start, the sooner you can leave."

That got her attention.

She angled her head slightly, curiosity getting the better of her. "What kind of weapon is it?"

"It's essentially a crossbow. With modifications. Magical ones. I came across a version of it once..." My hand clenched as I tried to bury the memory. "But it's gone now. Thanks to your abilities, I'll have one like it for my collection."

"Do you have a supplier?" She was so close to the window her breath fogged the glass.

"A supplier?"

"Of magic."

"Oh, yes. I have someone who owes me a favor."

Her tone was dry. "Did you threaten him too?"

I made a sound in the back of my throat. "They're a she…and what do you think?"

"I think we're here." Her lips parted as she gawked at the approaching manor perched near the edge of the cliff. The forest receded as we traveled down the rocky lane, and I tried to imagine the scene from her point of view. It didn't bode well. The three-story structure of dark, crumbling stone lay sprawled across a weed-infested, overgrown property. Ivy climbed the face of the manor and wound around giant pillars. Most of the lower windows had been boarded up, and a few of them had iron bars.

The carriage slowed to a stop just as the front door opened, and a lone woman stood in the entrance. I climbed from the carriage and held out my hand for Liana. She was slow to move, taking a moment to tuck the blade back into its sheath. Ignoring my offer of help, she exited onto the gravel driveway and wrapped her arms around her shoulders, either warding off the chill or the gloom projected from the manor.

"My housekeeper, Ms. Wilder, will help get you settled and show you to your workspace. Give her a list of personal items you require, and we'll have them delivered. Once you're situated, your work will begin.

And Liana?" I waited until her gaze met mine.

"Yes?" she whispered.

"Welcome home."

Chapter 6

Liana

Welcome home?
Neither word fit my situation or the monster of a house standing in front of me. It was badly neglected, and there was something oddly forlorn about its structure, almost as if it sat alone at the edge of the world. In the distance, the sheer face of a cliff gave way to a view of the horizon, and somewhere below, the surf crashed against the rocks.

The air tasted of salt and the hint of snow Bowen had mentioned in the carriage. My neck heated as embarrassment tipped the scale over fear. I hadn't had an attack like that in a long time, and I always hated the feeling afterward. The knowing stares. The pity.

Bowen's lame attempt at conversation was likely for my benefit. An attempt to diffuse the situation. He probably thought I was a lunatic! My lips trembled on a hysterical smile as I replayed his puzzled features. He'd made a joke about stabbing the upholstery, but he definitely thought my dagger was meant for him.

I did threaten him, so I guess I shouldn't be surprised.

I watched as he bounded up the cracked steps and spoke quietly with his housekeeper. She nodded once. Then he disappeared into the manor. There wasn't anything left to do but follow.

Climbing the manor's stairs, I tilted my head back as I crossed beneath the pillared archway. Vines choked the stone, and giant cracks made me question the soundness of the structure. The housekeeper ushered me inside the foyer. She had severe features, angular cheekbones, and hooded eyes set beneath thick brows. Her uniform was starched and her hair pulled back, yet she'd let a few ringlets loose around her ears, which gave her a somewhat youthful appearance.

"I'm Ms. Wilder. I run the manor and manage a small team of servants. As an employee here, you'll report directly to Lord MacKenzie, and then to myself for smaller issues. I'll show you to your room, and then I'll show you to your workspace." She bobbed her head in a curt nod, but then her features softened slightly, her mouth gracing me with a thin smile. "I realize the manor is quite intimidating, but it isn't a terrible place to work. Just follow the rules and don't touch anything." With that, she turned toward a massive mahogany staircase with ornate balusters and a giant branched lighting fixture made of wood and metal.

My room was on the third floor, and even though the outside of the manor was in major need of repair, the inside was fairly tidy and in good shape. At least the parts I could see. The dark-paneled walls gleamed beneath the light of wrought iron wall sconces, but with almost no natural light, the halls were shadowed and grim. Decorations ranged from woven tapestries depicting battle scenes to bronze shields affixed to the walls. A suit of armor was stationed on the third-floor landing, and I rushed past it, afraid it might reach out and snag my cloak with its metal fingers. I glanced over my shoulder to make sure it hadn't moved before continuing down the hall.

"Here we are." Ms. Wilder swung open a door and gestured inside with her hand.

I peered into the gaping blackness, and a bubble of panic lodged in my throat. Ms. Wilder strode into the room and pulled back a pair of heavy drapes, letting in a thin stream of meager light. She lit a candle, handed me the iron base, then proceeded to turn down the canopied bedsheets.

"It's lovely," I murmured weakly, taking stock of the unique furnishings and what appeared to be a second suit of armor tucked into the corner. The metal statue made my insides queasy. How was I supposed to sleep with *that thing* in here? Hopefully, it wasn't too heavy, and I could drag it into the hallway—or at the very least, make it face the wall.

Finished with her chore, Ms. Wilder clapped her hands and retreated from the room. "We'll have whatever personal items you require—clothes, toiletries, etcetera—delivered to your room. Meals are served thrice daily. You can take them in your room or your workshop, though Lord MacKenzie has also instructed you're welcome to use the dining hall if you wish."

I gazed back inside the bedroom. Unless I ate pressed up against the window, I wouldn't even be able to see my food.

"Come along, this way. It's time to head down to your workspace."

Ms. Wilder led me back to the first floor and then to the far end of the manor, where another staircase plunged us into a cavernous system of stone corridors. We passed an armory, various storage rooms, and a forge. At the end of the corridor was my workspace.

The housekeeper paused outside the door. "If you go back in the other direction, you'll find the antechamber to the gallery where Lord MacKenzie stores the vast majority of his collection." Her gaze narrowed with stern precision, and her tone grew dire. "You may look, but do not touch."

I nodded, sticking my hands behind my back, worried she might slap them preemptively. Ms. Wilder reached for the door handle, wincing a little before she accompanied me inside. A single grungy window set high near the ceiling let in a muted light. I raised the candle, my heart sinking at the appalling scene in front of me.

Bowen MacKenzie was a hoarder.

Crates of varying sizes were stacked almost to the rafters. Barrels used as mini tables were laden with rusted tools, piles of screws, and blocks of wood. The floor was covered in layers of dust and soot, and lengths of chain-link metal snaked the scuffed wooden beams, waiting to snag unsuspecting feet.

Every square inch of the wall was draped with some sort of hanging apparatus, all of which looked broken or ready to crumble from disuse. I moaned as my gaze landed on the main workbench, littered two feet deep with clutter, cans of paint, oil canisters, and stacks upon stacks of tattered parchment.

"Okay, well, if you need me, don't hesitate to pull the servant's bell in the main foyer. I'll leave you to get started." Her eyes were wide and her smile brittle. The woman couldn't wait to hightail it out of the pit of squalor where it appeared all things went to die. Who could blame her?

"Thank you," I mumbled, still dazed by the wretched workshop.

I felt a draft from her exit.

Expelling a long breath, I swept my hand across the worktable to make room for the candle. Somehow, my palm came away sticky, and I suppressed a shudder.

Nope. This won't do. This won't do at all.

***

"Move that rack of spears to the corner, please." I pointed to the space I'd spent all day clearing of clutter.

The man—Gavin, I believe was his name—grunted his disapproval but still bent to heft the heavy rack. When he only dragged it a few inches, he snapped his fingers at a waiting servant to grab the other end.

I nodded in satisfaction, surveying my progress over the past couple of days. The space might be a useable workshop when I was through with it. Gone were the crates and most of the junk. Anything that was even remotely rusted had been tossed or melted in the forge. The floor had been thoroughly dusted and scrubbed clean, and any item that didn't serve a purpose had been removed.

A few of the servants had graciously offered to help me with cleaning. I sensed their pity but didn't care so long as it came with two hands and a broom.

"What are you going to do with all these lanterns?" Gavin asked, studying the rows I'd lined up on the worktable.

"Hang them, of course. I'll chop my fingers off without proper lighting." Which was the truth, but it also served as a good excuse to cover my fear of the dark. So far, I'd been able to manage my anxiety, but the ever oppressive shadows were eating away at me.

He scrubbed a hand over his face and yawned deeply. "Have someone wake me when you need to use the ladder. I'm taking a nap until then." He took a final look around the workshop and mumbled under his breath, "Bowen is going to lose his mind."

The other servant followed him out of the room, leaving me alone in my freshly cleaned space. I groaned and stretched my arms overhead, my muscles screaming from the back-breaking work.

Since I arrived at the manor, my routine had consisted of eating, sleeping, and decluttering. There wasn't time to evaluate my situation or the elusive man who'd hired me. I'd only seen him a handful of times—once, to sign a contract detailing the terms of my indentured servitude. He'd watched with a pensive stare while I signed my name then dusted the ink with powder. Our bargain sealed, he'd folded the parchment and stored the contract in his desk.

Now, I waited on pins and needles for him to come down and survey the changes to his workshop and deliver the plans for the commission. Waiting was the worst. The longer it took, the more anxious I became.

And the more curious.

I'd picked up bits and pieces of trivia about him from the servants, matching them with the stories I'd heard in the village. I'd even spent a few hours in the gallery marveling over the rare artifacts and one-of-a-kind weapons in his collection. I only touched a few things, and the petty acts of defiance were worth the risk of getting caught. In truth, I did it on purpose, eager to see if the act would cause the master of the house to appear out of the dark like a fabled creature of the night.

It didn't, which only increased my raging curiosity.

The man was an enigma. A muscle-bound, brooding, striking enigma.

I shuffled toward the worktable, pressing my thumbs into my spine to relieve the tension. There were still piles of papers to sort through, and I hadn't even opened the drawers. Who knew what nightmare lived in those? Inhaling an uneasy breath, I reached for the drawer pull, praying to the God of Cleanliness they'd be empty.

They were not.

Inside was a stack of leather-bound journals. Removing the top one from the pile, I unwound the leather strap holding it together and set the journal on the worktable. I moved a lantern closer as I flipped through the pages.

Watercolor drawings covered the parchment, illustrating a few of the artifacts I'd seen in the gallery. They were vividly painted by a skillful hand, and I noted the slash of a signature in the corner.

Bowen.

I turned to the next page, fascinated by the drawing of a jeweled dagger. The depth and the shading made the image jump off the parchment, almost as if I could wrap my hand around the hilt. To say Bowen was a talented artist didn't do him justice. Slowly, I worked my way through the journal and on to the next one.

A twinge of guilt pinched my chest at the thought maybe I shouldn't be going through his personal belongings, but the journals had essentially been forgotten, buried inside drawers that had nearly rusted shut. I kept turning pages until I came to a series of drawings that made me pause. I read aloud the caption beneath the image.

"Incantus."

For some reason, the name sent an icy shiver down my back. The sketch was of a medallion with odd symbols carved into the surface. I didn't recognize any of the markings, but they gave me a bad feeling, as if the symbols were cursed and anyone viewing them would take the curse back with them.

Closing the journal, I shook away the unexplained dread. It was only a drawing. It didn't make any sense to be afraid of it.

Yet hours later, while I dined by candlelight alone in my room, I couldn't help but think about Bowen's beautiful sketches and the medallion that made me glad I wore a dagger on my hip.

Chapter 7

Bowen

Bitter coffee burned the roof of my mouth, scorching a fiery path down my throat. My mug landed on my desk, and dark liquid sloshed over the brim to stain the wood and papers beneath it. I blew out a breath and crossed to the window to stare out at the frozen landscape.

A light layer of snow had fallen during the night, dusting the ground in white powder. The icy chill penetrated the glass and sank into my bones. It was a perfect contradiction. Hot and cold. Two extremes that embodied my mood over the past few days since Liana arrived.

So far, things hadn't gone to plan. According to my housekeeper, she'd taken one look at her workspace and insisted on cleaning. Cleaning! For three days. She refused to start work on the commission until everything was in order. She'd directed the servants, commanding them to move this and that. The noise was endless, the sounds echoing through the cavernous manor. It was as if the house itself had woken from an endless slumber.

I turned from the window and retrieved my mug. Steam wafted from the rim, but I downed it anyway. The pain was a moment's distraction from a simple realization I'd been trying to avoid.

After three days, the house was quiet.

Too quiet.

Its usual tomblike atmosphere had never bothered me before. I preferred it. Reveled in it. But now, the silence grated. Liana's entire presence was a whirlwind to the senses. From the second she walked through the door, there'd been some kind of disturbance.

So why was it so quiet?

With my hand wrapped around my empty mug, I thumped it against the desk, only so I could hear the sound echo through the room. As if in answer, a pair of knuckles rapped against the doorframe, and I paused, my mug inches away from another beating.

"Why are you making so much noise?" Gavin muttered. "Some people are trying to sleep." He rubbed his bleary eyes and then slung his arms across his chest, his mouth firmly planted in a scowl.

"Have I disturbed your beauty sleep?" I mocked, matching his stance with a scowl of my own.

"Ah, I can see you're brooding more than usual. To what do we owe this displeasure?" Gavin ran a hand over the thick stubble covering his jawline. "Wait—don't answer. Let me guess. It's more fun that way."

"Get out, Gavin."

"Hmm...let's see. You're irritable—which doesn't reveal much considering it's a common occurrence."

He cocked his head as if in deep thought. "You're scowling—also common—and you're taking your aggression out on inanimate objects." He lounged against the wall. "You know, now that I think about it, you're not acting differently. It must be a Tuesday."

"It's Thursday."

Gavin scratched his head, and messy brown strands fell into his eyes. "Is it? I could have sworn it was Tuesday."

"You drink too much," I grumbled, tossing my mug back onto the desk.

Gavin rarely woke before lunchtime. If he hadn't cemented his friendship with me when we were younger, I would have already sent him packing. But after a rough year, he needed a place to stay—not to mention a few odd jobs to keep him occupied and flush with coin.

It helped we were kindred spirits. Gavin had demons of his own, ones he battled with liquor and too much sleep. I'd chosen seclusion. Nothing but silence and solitude. And look where that had gotten me.

Chuckling, Gavin entered the room and lowered himself into a chair. "How else am I supposed to make the days blur? I prefer numbness to mimicking your raging hostility. There's only room for one beast in this castle, and you were here first."

"Lucky me."

"I'd say you're pretty lucky. I paid a visit to your new employee." He made a face, scrunching his features. "She made me move a rack of iron spears. It was heavy. I may have twisted something in my neck." A slow grin replaced his annoyance as he massaged the tendons. "But you never mentioned she was so beautiful."

I braced my knuckles on the desk and leaned forward, trying to smother the burst of irritation at Gavin's accurate but unsolicited observation. "Whether or not she's beautiful has no bearing on her talent. I would have brought her here even if her face were as ugly as yours."

Gavin scoffed. "Impossible. I've been told repeatedly in the past that I'm a handsome man. Look at this chiseled jawline." He turned his head, showing me his profile. "And my nose. It may have been broken a few times, but that only showcases my rugged strength."

"Yeah, well, be careful around my new employee, or you may find your nose broken again."

"By you or her?"

Good question. My knuckles pressed so hard against the desktop they began to ache. "What are you doing up here this early?" I asked.

Gavin stretched his neck, cringing from the pain as he tilted his head. "It's been a couple of days since she arrived. I figured I should check to see if Liana made good on her threat and murdered you in your sleep. I'd hate to be out of a job."

My scowl deepened. "Because any normal position would require you to get up with the sun."

"Don't joke about things like that." Gavin shuddered and clutched the side of his head.

"Why are you really here, darkening my office doorstep looking like death warmed-over?"

He smirked at my description, taking a small amount of pride in it. "Because I thought you should know the word is out that the Grimm's blade never made it to its final destination. Argus Ward knows it's missing. It's only a matter of time until he tracks it here. He's working with an oracle."

I went still.

Argus Ward.

Hearing his name made my scars itch.

He needed the blade I'd secured from the merchants, and I planned to draw him here to exact my revenge. Would seeing his face when he realized I'd taken from him what he desired most be enough to ease my misery? It would have to be. Argus had taken everything from me, and while he wasn't the one to deliver my scars, his actions had led to them.

He'd never suffered for those actions.

His fortune had thrived, his business prospered, while my opportunities had withered, my reputation as scarred as my body. Making him pay was the only thing that mattered.

Misery for misery. It was all I had left.

Gavin had grown quiet, waiting for my reaction, when above our heads the floor groaned. I followed Gavin's gaze to the ceiling. There was a loud thud, accompanied by the prolonged screech of wood scraping across wood.

"Looks as if someone else is awake." Gavin grimaced at another horrific thud. "You should probably make sure your new employee isn't trying to jump out the window."

I grunted and strode past him into the hallway. Taking the stairs to the third floor, I made my way toward Liana's room. Wasn't I just complaining about the quiet making me miserable? Now there was noise, and I was anxious. What was that woman up to? The thuds went silent, so I picked up my pace, dread mixing with curiosity. If I found her underneath a toppled bureau...

Glass shattered, and I broke into a dead run.

Reaching her door, I halted long enough to question the suit of armor stationed outside her room. One of the metal arms was bent at an odd angle, and the helmet was askew. *What in the devil...?* I twisted the handle, not bothering to knock. The door swung inward, and I squinted against a stream of harsh sunlight pouring in from the far window.

A muffled curse caught my attention. I dragged my gaze to the other side of the room. Liana stood on her toes, a rickety end table beneath her feet. Her arms were outstretched, fingers attempting to snag the curtain rod that was an inch out of her reach.

"What the hell are you doing?" I barked.

She whirled, surprise shifting to panic as the table rocked. Her arms flailed, eyes going wide as her body swerved toward the edge.

Time seemed to slow as I lunged through the doorway. My boots skidded over shards of glass, trying to reach her in time.

The full length of her crashed into me, and my

hands banded around her waist. Liana's thick hair covered my face, making it impossible to see. I would have laughed at our awkward position if I weren't still reeling from seeing her nearly take a swan dive onto the floor.

She was off-balance, so I picked her up, swinging her legs over my forearm. Her head shook back and forth as she tried to dislodge the flowing strands of hair tangled in her eyes. The blonde waves moved on puffs of air.

Was she still cursing?

Yup, definitely cursing.

"What is wrong with you?" she sputtered, finally shoving the hair away from her mouth. "Are you trying to kill me?" Her eyes spat fire, and she squirmed in my arms like a vicious cat trying to get free.

"Quit moving! There's glass everywhere, and you aren't wearing shoes."

She went still, her gaze dropping to her bare feet then to the glass glittering across the floorboards. "I broke the lantern," she mumbled without a hint of apology. "The blasted thing slipped out of my hands when I tried to climb onto the table."

I lifted her higher against my chest to get a better hold. "And what were you doing on the table?"

She made a face as if the answer should be obvious and gestured wildly toward the windows. "I was tearing down the curtains!"

"What? Why?"

"Because it's too dark in here even when they're pulled back. I don't like it, and I couldn't take it anymore. This room may be well-furnished, but it's as dark as a crypt. Ever heard of natural lighting?"

"Ever heard of asking? I suppose that answers my question about the suit of armor. You must have moved him too, busted his arm while you were at it." Stepping out of the glass field, I strode toward the bed and tossed her onto the mattress.

Her temper spiked as she bounced clumsily on the wide surface. She let out another curse and jabbed her finger into the air once she'd gained her equilibrium.

"Do you have any idea what it's like trying to sleep with a weird, lifelike tin statue staring at you from the corner? It's terrifying."

I ducked my head to conceal an amused smile and searched the floor for her shoes. I found them hiding under the bed and dug them out.

"Put these on. I'll have someone come clean the glass and remove the statue. And check with me next time you want to do a little reorganizing." I walked toward the window with the remaining curtain and yanked it free, dodging the metal rod that fell with it.

Liana stuffed her feet into her shoes and stepped quickly over the glass to reach her belt lying on top of the bureau. With the curtains gone, light framed her back, making her blonde hair glow in a halo of sunshine. She attached the belt to her waist, taking a second to check the sheathed dagger. She carried it with her everywhere. Probably ate her meals with it, and I wouldn't be shocked if she slept with it too.

Such strange habits...

"Let's go," I said, crooking my finger. "I'll have your

breakfast sent down to the workshop, and then I'm going to show you the plans for your commission. Meet me there in twenty minutes."

A spark of interest flickered in her gaze, but it faded as she chewed the corner of her lip. "Uh, about your workshop…"

"What about my workshop?"

She stalled, toying with a long strand of her hair. It looked as if she were about to answer, then she changed her mind. "Oh, nothing. But you're welcome to bring me the plans here. There's no need for you to go all the way down—"

"My workshop. Twenty minutes."

Chapter 8

Liana

"Twenty minutes," I mimicked with a snarl. I paced the floor of the workshop, stopping mid-stride to survey the room. Nerves churned in my stomach. Maybe he wouldn't mention the changes.

Ms. Wilder had dropped off a breakfast tray, removed the lid on the steaming pile of eggs and toast, and then hurried from the room as if there were an animal on her heels. Her deliberate flight made me wary of my upcoming encounter with Bowen.

He was going to be mad. I probably shouldn't have thrown out all of his tools. I picked at the toast and brushed the crumbs from my fingers. No—they all had to go. Besides, there was nothing in the contract that said I couldn't make the place my own. I may only be at the manor a short while, but that was no reason to work in filth.

I mean, sure, he lost his temper a bit when he caught me tearing down the curtains in my room, but I'd like to think it had more to do with me falling off the table than his love for the gloomy drapery.

Cringing, I rubbed the back of my neck. If only I could stop showing him all of my weak spots. First the panic attack in the carriage, and now the curtain debacle. At least he finally planned to show me the commission he'd hired me for. I'd be able to prove myself in that respect—though why I was so determined to have him see me in a good light was beyond me. The man was rude and ill-natured. Not to mention, a brute. He had some nerve tossing me like a sack of potatoes onto the mattress. I huffed a breath and silenced the devil on my shoulder whispering about the dangers of broken glass on bare feet.

"He could have been gentle about it," I grumbled.

"Gentle about what?"

The rough timbre of his voice made me spin toward the door. Bowen stood in the entrance. His arms were braced across his chest like wooden beams, and a scowl hardened his mouth. He held a scroll in his hand, and there was a pen tucked behind his ear, giving his menacing stance an almost studious undercurrent.

Great, now he's caught me talking to myself.

"Nothing. I was just—"

"What have you done?" He strode into the room, uninterested in my rambling answer. Raking a hand through his hair, he blinked at the empty walls. "Where are all my things? My tools? My—"

"Your tools were rusted. Unusable at best, dangerous at worst. I organized everything else and moved most of the clutter into the adjoining space. Oh, and I dusted. Nearly sneezed myself into a coma,"

I said, muttering the last part under my breath.

"You strung lanterns?" His gaze followed the string of hanging lanterns stretching from one end of the room to the other. A few others hung from chains affixed to the ceiling. He weaved through them, ducking to keep from banging his head against the metal bases.

"Um, yes."

His brow arched. "Let me guess—it was too dark in here."

I straightened my spine and gave him a sarcastic smile. "Proper lighting is essential."

"So I'm learning." He placed the scroll onto the workbench and unfurled the ends. Reaching for a pedestal candle to keep the scroll taut, he paused, his attention caught on the stack of leather-bound drawings. The scroll whirled back together as he rounded the table toward the drawings.

"Where did you find these?" he rasped, gathering them up against his chest as if I hadn't already pored over each one for hours.

"I found them buried inside the drawers of the worktable. They're yours, right? I think they're wonderful."

He flexed his fingers, and a little of the fight drained out of him. "They're just sketches. They're not worth anything."

"Well, I like them. Do you have more?"

His features clouded over. "I haven't drawn in a long time." He didn't elaborate and returned to where he'd left the scroll. "I believe this is the last piece I sketched."

I bent over the drawing and moved a candle closer. The crossbow was depicted in vivid detail, a mixture of metal and wood complete with dimensions. At the end of the grooved track where the bolt resided was a cylindrical tube enclosing a blue flame. I recognized the magic modification immediately. Ice bolts. The blue flame trapped in the cylinder produced a continual reaction that fired freezing arrows.

"This is incredible. I haven't come across a bow like this before. You said you've seen one? Where?"

"A few years ago. I was on one of my last treasure hunts and came across this weapon in a tomb. I recovered it and brought it back along with the artifacts I was hired to find. I planned to add it to my collection, but it was stolen from me." His voice lowered. "Along with everything else."

"I'm sorry." I traced my finger over the trigger and then up to the rail. "What is this hollow section in the bolt for?"

Bowen leaned closer and wrapped his warm fingers over mine, guiding my hand from the blue flame to the hollow groove. "When the trigger is pulled, a trace amount of magic infuses the compartment. When the bolt strikes its target, the blue flame is injected, causing whatever it hits to freeze. A field, a lake, even an enemy."

Despite the warmth emanating from his skin, I shivered, imagining such a brutal cold. "And your magic supplier can acquire a blue flame? They're rare for a reason."

He let go of my fingers, though his gaze seemed to linger on them, sliding up my palm to the visible birthmark on my wrist that signaled my gift. "Can you transfer this type of magic?"

"Of course."

"Then my supplier can get it."

I studied the drawing again, a sliver of anticipation sliding through my body. It had been a while since I'd created something so unique. You can get sick of working with enchanted steel. Everyone always wants to get their hands on an enchanted blade, but they're actually pretty boring.

This, however? This was a challenge. A type of magic I hadn't handled before. My favorite kind. His request shouldn't have surprised me though. Bowen was a collector of the rarest artifacts, and a collection like his could speak volumes of the man who assembled it.

"I have to ask, what is it about weapons that appeals to you so much?"

He was slow to respond. The shadows from the hanging lanterns danced across his face. It occurred to me I might not like his explanation, yet I waited anxiously, wondering if it would match my own.

"I admire the skill in the craftsmanship."

I frowned. The answer itself wasn't disappointing —I relished in the creative process myself—but it felt like a surface revelation. It didn't dig deep enough.

He must have read my disapproval because he asked, "You don't like my answer?"

"Is it the truth?"

His thumb found my chin, lifting it until our gazes locked. "It's a half-truth. Most people don't like to hear the rest."

I swallowed, held captive by him in a way I wasn't used to. "I'm not most people."

"No, you're not." He dropped his hand but leaned in with the rest of his body until my back was pressed against the edge of the workbench. He was going for intimidation, testing me against his assumptions of society. If I retreated, I failed. If I was appalled by whatever words spilled from his lips, I failed.

Somehow, I knew I wouldn't fail.

"It's true I find beauty in the craftsmanship, but there's also something seductive in the purpose." The thumb that touched my chin now trailed the surface of an unmolded bar of steel sitting on the workbench. "To have an object that gives you power over another is significant, because often, power is taken from us. It can be a test of will to surround yourself with that power and keep it in check when everything inside you begs you to let it loose."

My gaze roamed over his scars. "That sounds bloodthirsty."

"Maybe I am."

The soft rasp of his voice made my breath catch. He didn't realize it, but we'd found equal footing. I too had felt powerless, stripped of my freedom, and instilled with the desire to never let it happen again.

"That's the answer I was looking for."

He studied me for a long moment with an expression I couldn't decipher. Finally, he shook his head as if clearing his thoughts and stepped back. His throat cleared.

"Now that you've gotten the place in order and know what needs to be done, I should leave you to your work. Make a list of items you'll need, and any tools." His sharp gaze found mine on that one, and I had the decency to look guilty. "I'll handle the rest."

He left me with the scroll and crossed the room, slowing near the entrance. His hesitation made me curious, and I caught him shaking his head again, almost as if he were trying to come to a decision.

"Was there something else?" I asked.

"I realize it's a lot to ask to be trapped down here all day." He paused, and I could see those warring emotions on his face again. "Anyway, I thought since you're so obsessed with optimal lighting, you might want to take a break in the training room this afternoon. Say, two o'clock? Ms. Wilder can give you directions. I think you'll enjoy it."

I gave a cautious nod.

Bowen hesitated another second and then thumped his fist lightly against the stone wall. "All right then. See you this afternoon."

***

The morning passed slowly. I kept replaying our conversation over and over, and I lost count of the times I stared off into space, imagining the rough pad of this thumb against my skin when he lifted my gaze to his. If I wasn't careful, I'd end up with a hole in the hand or a third-degree burn.

Shaking the images from my mind, I stretched my arms over my head and glanced at the timepiece sitting on the workbench. I'd been working for hours, developing a plan and making preparations for the job ahead. I'd even cycled through his stack of drawings again, fascinated by their detail and pure artistry.

Now, it was nearly two o'clock. Did I dare accept Bowen's invitation?

The rational part of me told me to keep working. Taking breaks would only slow the process and keep me from returning home. I eyed the slight knick on my finger caused by one of my distracted fantasies and came to a decision. Breaks were rational too—for safety.

I put the few remaining tools away and wiped down the workbench. The clock inched closer to two, and I picked up my pace, extinguishing the lanterns one by one. Satisfied with the state of the workshop, I left to find Ms. Wilder.

The housekeeper was in the kitchen preparing a tray. She poured milk from a pitcher into a tall glass. Next to the glass was a small plate of cookies. The scent of chocolate chips made my mouth water, and I eyed the plate with amusement. Did Bowen have a sweet tooth? Either way, it was another surprising tidbit that didn't fit in with his villainous reputation.

"Take this with you to the training room," Miss Wilder said, handing me the tray. "Go up to the third floor, east wing. All the way at the end of the hall, you'll find a door leading to a spiral staircase. Hurry, before the cookies cool." She ushered me from the kitchen with a dismissive wave, and I followed her directions until I found the spiral staircase.

I peered up the shadowy passage. Candles flickered in sconces affixed to the walls, and an iron handrail swirled above the steps. A nervous ache tightened my chest at the narrowed space, but I pushed back the fear and started to climb.

"I thought he said there'd be optimal light," I grumbled, pausing at the halfway point to rebalance the tray.

At the top, I walked down a short corridor and emerged onto a platform that expanded into a large glass-enclosed dome. Sunshine poured into the room, and I squinted against the abrupt change in lighting until my vision acclimated.

It was incredible. The dome overlooked the entire estate, and I saw the crystal-blue ocean on the horizon. A few of the windows had been vented, allowing fresh air to filter in, and I drew in a deep breath, filling my lungs. It was cold but refreshing.

Around the perimeter of the dome, glass cases displayed various items from Bowen's collection. Strange artifacts and jeweled boxes sparkled in the bright light. In the center of the space was a large mat where a boy of maybe twelve or thirteen practiced with a saber modified for his size. Bowen observed the boy, issuing a series of increasingly difficult commands. At his feet, watching with lazy, unamused eyes, was a giant dog.

I rested the tray on my hip, impressed as the boy dodged an imaginary adversary. His wheat-blond hair glinted in the sun and fell into his eyes on his next lunge.

In an instant, my throat closed as his features morphed into my brother's. At least, the image of my brother from before our captivity, when he was flush with health and a ready smile.

The soles of the boy's shoes squeaked across the mat, jarring me from the memory, and I moved closer, placing the tray onto a wooden bench. I realized who the cookies were for, and a smile crested my lips.

This place was full of surprises.

Bowen noticed my presence and gestured me forward. The boy lowered the end of his saber and bowed. The dog upstaged them both, jumping to his feet, his tail wagging in frantic excitement. He thrust his snout into my leg, making me shift my weight to keep from falling over. Bowen steadied my elbow.

"Sit, Brutus."

The dog didn't listen and wagged his tail harder.

Bowen sighed. "This is Brutus. I found him wandering the grounds a while back and took him in. He's an evil thing and extremely dangerous."

Brutus licked the back of my hand when I bent to stroke the fur behind his ear.

"See? He's practically a monster." He indicated the boy. "And this is Jacob Carver. He's the stable boy. I let him train up here after he completes his duties. He also has a fascination with weapons." Bowen winked. "But he doesn't care about the craftsmanship. He's only interested in fighting. Jacob, meet Liana Archer."

Jacob grinned and bowed for a second time. "It's a

pleasure to meet you, Miss Archer."

Nodding, I offered him a timid smile, still recovering from seeing the likeness of my brother. Jacob patted his thighs, trying to call Brutus back to the mat. The dog looked up at me with adoring eyes and sat down at my feet.

I stifled a smile. I didn't expect to find a child, let alone a dog, inside Bowen's house. Nothing seemed to match Bowen's reputation. Not this room in the sky, not the young boy with the friendly grin, nor the harmless dog resting his head against my toes. Yet I knew something was lurking beneath the surface. A darkness he couldn't escape. A pain he'd hinted at earlier, in the workshop.

It was strange to see so much of myself reflected back at me. My scars may not be on the outside for everyone to see, but they were there.

I lifted my foot from underneath Brutus's snout and stepped onto the mat, reaching for Jacob's saber. "Do you mind?"

Jacob shook his head, allowing me to adjust his grip around the hilt.

I placed both hands on his shoulders, moving him into place. "You have an excellent technique, but when you lunge, place your center of gravity here."

He flashed me an astonished smile as he deepened the move with more control than he had before. "Miss Archer, do you enjoy fighting?"

I ruffled the hair near his ear, noting the ache in my chest as my fingers sifted through the soft strands. I sighed. "No, Jacob. I don't enjoy fighting. I enjoy winning."

Before he could react to my statement, I hooked my ankle around his and jerked him off-balance. The grip on his saber loosened, and I swung my arm out to snatch it from his hand. Lowering into a fighting stance, I grinned at his wide-eyed expression.

His mouth parted in an awed circle. "You have to teach me that move, Miss Archer."

I returned the saber and shrugged. "To be honest, it's not so much the move that makes overcoming your opponent possible; it's recognizing the other person's lack of faith in your ability. Had you known, you might have had your guard up. Never let your opponent take you by surprise." I wagged my finger. "But better yet, always assume everyone is an opponent."

We both jumped as Bowen threw back his head and laughed. The booming sound echoed through the dome, and Jacob's eyes grew wider than when I disarmed him.

"Now you've done it, Miss Archer. You've really done it."

"Done what?" My voice sounded strained as Bowen stopped laughing and stalked closer, prowling to the center of the mat. The heat from his gaze could have melted the frost on the glass.

Jacob thrust the saber back into my hand. "You've amused the beast."

Chapter 9

Bowen

Very little surprised me anymore. People acted according to predetermined notions, and I prided myself on always being one step ahead. It was one of the things that made me a great treasure hunter: I'd honed the ability to know when someone was leading me down the wrong path. But Liana was a puzzle I'd only started to solve.

The tiniest curve of her lips alerted me to her true intentions. It would have been easy to miss, and I wasn't sure any good would come from watching her so closely. Not that I had much of a choice. She owned the room. The brightest thing in a room full of sunshine.

Selecting a matching saber from the training rack, I weighed it in my hands. A thrill of anticipation shot through me as I stepped onto the mat. Jacob scurried out of my path. He sank onto the viewing bench and stuffed a cookie into his mouth, watching with rapt attention. Brutus settled beneath him, catching the crumbs as they fell.

I raised the tip of the saber in a challenge,

my brow arched. "And this morning, you called me bloodthirsty."

A flush painted her cheeks. "You admitted it freely."

"I would have admitted it sooner if I'd known you felt the same way." The corner of my mouth twitched. "Be straight with me, Liana. You enjoy letting people read you the wrong way. You use it to your advantage."

Her eyes flared as I paced closer. She bit the side of her lip, worrying it between her teeth. Indecision lasted only a moment before she lifted her blade in response. The tip pressed against my jacket. If I took another step, it would meet my heart. The steadiness of her grip should have alarmed me, but it only made me want to move closer and put her to the test.

"You do the same thing," she countered.

"Do I? Then what am I leading you to believe right now?"

She narrowed her gaze. "You're leading me to believe I have the upper hand in this situation."

"You don't think you do? There's a blade ruining my jacket that says otherwise."

"But you're not nervous. You're still moving closer." She stepped back on her heel to keep from lodging the saber in my rib cage when I did exactly that.

I laughed softly. "What's one more scar when you already have so many?"

"Stop deflecting! You're trying to distract me."

"Is it working?"

"No." She scoffed and angled her head up a notch. "Then how come you're about to run into that glass case?"

A crease marred her brow as she reached behind her with her empty hand. There was no glass case, but the action made her lose focus just enough that her saber dipped. I took advantage, darting forward in an attack.

Quick to recover, she parried the blow, and steel struck steel. She rolled her wrist and advanced, thrusting her blade at an angle. I evaded the move, grinning wide as our blades met again. The clash echoed through the dome.

She puffed out a breath, lifting a curl of hair that had fallen into her eyes. "You don't play fair, sir."

"The bloodthirsty never do."

"Still, I'm nothing but a meek woman playing at swords." The sparkle in her eyes and the mockery in her tone said otherwise. She feinted left, then lunged.

I matched her stance and blocked her thrust. Our blades locked together.

Jacob crowed from the sidelines. He stuffed the last cookie into his mouth and cheered around the mouthful. Liana learned her lesson and ignored him. Her eyes delved into mine with such precision it seemed as if she could see beyond them to the secrets lying beneath.

She was making a calculation; judging her next move.

The air crackled with tension, and my heart drummed against my ribs from the thrill of seeing her in action. She was a worthy opponent, and I craved to see what she'd do next.

Her chest rose and fell in rapid breaths, and for a moment, we were motionless, caught inside some elusive pull.

"How are we going to determine a winner?" she asked.

My gaze dipped to her mouth. "Easy. You can admit I have the upper hand and declare me the winner."

Defiance flashed across her features at my smug answer. She had no intention of letting me win. Withdrawing a step, she moved back into a fighting stance, but her sly smile had me on edge. She was up to something.

Her attack happened so quickly I almost didn't counter it. My saber hissed through the air. Then, at the last second, she pivoted, dropping her blade low. With dawning horror at her intent, I tried to pull back, but it was too late. The edge of my blade grazed the skin below her elbow. Blood welled instantly, soaking through her sleeve.

She didn't make a sound.

My weapon dropped to the floor, thudding into the mat. White noise clouded my head as I reached for her arm.

Her lips quirked in the same way they did before she knocked Jacob off his feet. It was a trick. Kicking my saber out of reach, she advanced, pressing the tip of her blade against my chest where it had been when this whole game started. Except this time, I was unarmed and at her mercy.

"You lose, Bowen. But you're right about one thing: I do enjoy letting people read me the wrong way, and I use it to my advantage."

There was something in her tone. A little of that darkness she tried so hard to hide. Blood dripped down her arm, yet she didn't give it a second thought.

I couldn't take my eyes off her wound, and my hands clenched with the disgusted knowledge I'd put it there; she'd played me. The two emotions warred together until I couldn't tell which was stronger.

Jacob moved from the bench. "Does it hurt, Miss Archer?"

Brutus whined and nudged his nose against Liana's thigh in an attempt to offer comfort.

She shrugged, finally taking stock of her injury. "It looks worse than it is."

"It will scar."

The rasp in my tone seemed to surprise her, and she lifted her eyes to mine, visibly swallowing. "Then I guess we'll match."

I went still, her words washing over me. Who was this woman? And what kind of person put themselves in harm's way to prove a point?

"I have some bandages in my office. Come with me, and let's clean your wound."

Offering the saber to Jacob, she gave him an encouraging smile. "Let me know if you ever want to practice."

The boy nodded with vigor, enamored beyond belief.

He wasn't the only one.

She gave the training dome a wistful glance, doing that thing she did, angling her head to soak up the light as if it might be the last she would ever see. Then she followed me down the spiral staircase toward my office.

I pushed open the solid wood door, and the first thing I noticed was the heavy curtains. The room was blanketed in shadow, and my mind flashed to our earlier encounter in her room and then the other day in the carriage.

She didn't like the dark.

Mumbling under my breath, I stalked toward the drapes and ripped them down.

Her lips pressed together, but I caught a slight tremble as if she were concealing a smile. "You don't have to tear down all your curtains. I can manage."

I cleared my throat and felt heat climb up my neck. "It's not that. These blasted things haven't been washed in ages." I made a show of sniffing the fabric, then I bundled the curtains into a ball and tossed them into the hallway.

She bobbed her head and surveyed the room, not looking convinced by my excuse.

Crossing to my desk, I rifled through the drawers until I located a box of bandages. Unwinding a length of gauze, I waved her over.

"Let me see your arm."

Liana rolled up her sleeve past her elbow, wincing as the fabric slid over her cut. I pressed a strip of gauze against the wound to stem the trickle of blood. Her teeth clenched.

"Want a shot of whiskey for the pain?"

A laugh burst from her throat. "If you're offering,

I'll take the entire bottle."

Keeping the strip of gauze in place, I wound a clean bandage around her arm. "I thought you said it looks worse than it is."

"I take it back. It hurts like the devil. But I'm still glad I won." She made a pained face when I tied a knot in the bandage.

"You shouldn't have done that. It was dangerous and a stupid way to prove a point."

She didn't answer, letting my lecture hang in the air. With her wound bandaged, she grew curious again, wandering the perimeter of the room while I put away the supplies. Pausing in front of a shelving unit, she leaned close, studying a collection of stone statues I'd picked up while raiding a famous tomb. They'd been the first line of defense in a trap-laden tunnel and had nearly cost me an eye.

"Don't touch those!" I snapped, jabbing a finger at the ugly-looking sculptures.

Glancing over her shoulder at me, she wrinkled her nose. "I'm not an idiot, Bowen. I know a fury statue when I see one. After the cut on my arm, the last thing I need is a bolt through the head." Her gaze returned to the statue. "Speaking of, what size bolt does it carry? And where did you find these? They're extremely rare."

"What is it with you and staring down death?" I murmured, reaching over her shoulder to grip the statue at its base and place it on a higher shelf. Even if she stood on her toes, she'd be out of range of its firing trajectory.

Caged between my body and the shelves, she turned to face me. A glossy wave of her hair brushed against my jacket. Without thinking, my fingers gently trailed up her arm, ghosting past the injury I inflicted.

Her eyes flared. "Don't collect deadly things if you don't want people to stare at them."

"People stare at me all the time. Why should my collection be any different?"

Her gaze dipped to the scar running along my collarbone, then it traveled the path up the side of my face, lingering near my cheekbone.

My throat tightened. "They look worse than they are," I said, using her words.

A strange moment passed, and she stared at me in the same way she stared at the statues: knowing she shouldn't touch them, but drawn in all the same. She inhaled a breath and lifted her hand. I caught her wrist an inch from my face and felt the heat of her palm.

"What are you doing?"

Uncertainty clouded her gaze, and I wasn't even sure she knew. I released her wrist, letting her decide. Liana's hand hovered in the air before she brought her fingertips to the imperfection on my jawline, tracing it lightly with her nails.

"See? You aren't as deadly as your statues, and these aren't so bad."

"Don't you dare tell me my face has character," I grumbled, trying not to lean into her hand.

"Never that. You'd probably challenge me to a

duel."

I couldn't help it. I cracked a smile. Which was probably the first time I'd ever smiled while someone studied my scars.

"No more duels for you today. Besides, you should get some rest. We're heading into town tomorrow."

"We are?" Surprise parted her lips.

"Yes. We're going to visit my magic supplier. Once you have what you need, and if you're as good as you say you are, you'll be returning home in no time."

Her hand dropped to her side. "Right. The sooner the better."

I stepped back, putting some distance between us. My words sounded hollow to my ears. Maybe because I knew them for the lies they were. I'd already framed her father and had him thrown in jail to get her here. Now she was in my home, a beautiful mix of contradictions and secrets, the question became: What wouldn't I do to keep her here?

Chapter 10

Liana

"We're not taking the carriage?" I climbed down the stone steps, staring at the pair of horses stamping their feet in the driveway.

"I thought you'd prefer to ride into town. It's cold, but the sun's out," Bowen said, handing me the reins to a beautiful chestnut horse.

He had dressed fully in black again, the same as he was the day I first saw him. Dark riding gloves encased his fingers, and the hood from his cloak created deep shadows over his face. He seemed to wear the color like a suit of armor, using it to intimidate, but also to shield himself beneath it.

The gesture to ride into town may have seemed small to some, but I noted the struggle it must have been for him. Traveling in a carriage allowed him obscurity, and he'd offered to trade that in for my comfort at the expense of his own.

"I would prefer to ride, thank you."

Bowen offered his hand to help me mount the horse, and I took it, sliding up into the saddle. The sun felt wonderful on my face, so I tilted my head back to breathe in the fresh, salty air. I leaned into the horse, nudging my heels until we took off at a gallop.

After days of being cooped up inside the manor, riding across the countryside felt exhilarating and almost reminded me of being back home. Bowen seemed to be enjoying it too. He was a skilled rider and seemed more at ease atop the horse than he had inside the shadowy carriage. Bowen might consider obscurity a necessity, but it was clear a part of him longed to be unshackled by whatever demons held him captive.

We slowed as we neared the congested streets in town. Bowen took the lead, navigating us toward the market district.

It was years since I'd traveled these streets, yet somehow, it all seemed familiar. Things never change as much as they should. There were still impoverished merchants hawking their wares from beneath tattered awnings, and youngsters running rampant, searching for their next meal. Even the smells were the same: sizzling meats, fresh fish, and the acrid scent of spices, all with the tinge of unwashed bodies and desperation.

I followed Bowen down one side street then another, until we came to an arched doorway set into a stone building. There was no indication it was a shop of any kind. No signage and no windows to peer through at the merchandise. The place was deserted, and we were far enough from the main road I couldn't hear street noise.

"This is it," he said, helping me dismount.

"Are you sure?" I asked while he tied our horses up to a lone hitching post. "It's just a hole in the wall."

A breeze whipped through the alley, forcing me to pull the hood of my cloak over my head as its icy fingers froze the back of my neck. Rubbing my hands together for warmth, I peered at the solid wooden door. A giant metal ring serving as a knocker had been affixed in the center.

My lips quirked. "Let me guess—there's a secret knock to get inside."

"Very funny. This is a reputable establishment." Bowen approached the door and lifted the iron ring. He let it fall against the wood, waited three seconds, then knocked twice in rapid succession.

I muttered under my breath while we waited for someone to answer, "That sounded like a secret knock to me,"

The door creaked open, and we stepped inside a small vestibule leading directly to a staircase. I blinked, searching the space for whoever had opened the door. Bowen repressed a smirk at my confused expression.

"Magic," he whispered, placing his hand at the small of my back and urging me up the staircase.

"Creepy," I countered.

The stairs groaned with each step, and I held onto the railing until we reached the landing. At the top, we stopped in front of another door. This time, Bowen didn't knock, but he had to duck beneath the doorframe to enter.

Inside, soft, muted light filtered in from skylights and cast glowing pools across the floorboards. The shop was cozy and infused with the scent of sandalwood and rose water. Rows and rows of shelves displayed strange objects and trinkets while other wares hung from the low ceiling.

A woman flung back a ruby-and-gold tasseled curtain connected to an adjoining room and approached the counter. She had thick waves of luxurious black hair and flawless skin. Her hazel eyes were heavily fringed with dark lashes, and her mouth was wide and full. She smiled coyly at Bowen and leaned her elbows on the counter. Her luscious hair flowed around her shoulders, and she toyed with the ends, wrapping the locks around her fingers.

"Hey, stranger," she purred. "It's been a while."

"Have you been staying out of trouble, Cora?"

"Trouble finds me, Bowen. You know that." She winked. "What brings you to my shop?"

"We need a supply of magic. Something rare." Bowen crossed his arms and gave her a withering look. "Price is no object so long as you're discreet."

"I'm always a model of discretion." Cora pouted and picked at the back of her manicured nails. "You can't blame me for that time in Andovia. We were being questioned by pirates if you remember."

Bowen frowned. "I remember one of those pirates slipping you a jeweled pendant from their stash, and you sang like a canary."

She huffed a breath and tossed her hair over her shoulder. "We escaped, didn't we? You always get so hung up on the details." Her gaze flickered over me in an almost dismissive manner, yet I sensed a profound interest. "By the way, who's your friend?"

"Don't you worry about—"

"Liana Archer." I stepped forward and stuck out my hand, tired of being the third wheel in their trip down memory lane. Maybe it was petty, but I didn't like the way she eyed me as if I were a trivial bystander. I was... well, Bowen's employee, and that should count for something!

"It's a pleasure," Cora murmured in a tone that told me it clearly wasn't.

She eyed my hand, but didn't take it. Which was fine by me. I'd known her for mere minutes, and already, the feeling was mutual. There was a distinctly selfish aura about her, and given the tidbits of their past, she was the kind of person who'd willingly sacrifice her friends if it meant saving her skin—or in her case, scoring a jeweled pendant.

"As Bowen mentioned, we're here to purchase a supply of magic. I'll need to test the product before we finalize the sale. Make sure it's strong enough and not intentionally diluted. It happens more often than you think."

Cora bristled at my insinuation. "Aren't you a little young to be playing with magic? Bowen, she's cute, but it's obvious she's trying to pull one over on you. How much are you paying her?"

"You don't believe I can sense magic?"

At my challenge, Cora placed two objects on the counter. One was a glowing orb about the size of a peach pit, and the other was a smooth stone, the kind you'd find washed ashore by the waves.

"Pick one," she said, a cocky smile curling her lips.

Studying both objects, I rolled up my sleeves and reached for the stone, running my fingertips over its satiny surface. My brow creased in concentration. The stone was cool to the touch. I set it aside and picked up the orb, enclosing it in my fist. The glow vanished behind my fingers, and the orb seemed to warm in my palm. My eyes drifted shut, and I exhaled long and deep. When I opened my eyes, I unfurled my fingers and held out the orb.

Cora lifted a sculpted brow. "I've already sold three of those orbs this week to three very gullible customers. No one ever chooses the stone. I didn't think you would either. Bowen, she's a charlatan."

"I didn't select it because it's just a stone. There's no magic in it."

She laughed softly. "You're right, but I like to use it as a test."

"I can see that. You use the stone as a decoy knowing everyone will choose the glowing orb. But there's no magic in either object. It's all a ruse." I dropped the orb back on the counter.

Her smirk faltered.

"Is she telling the truth, Cora?" Bowen's deep voice sounded over my shoulder. Amusement lurked in his tone.

A frown pinched her mouth, and she reached beneath the counter to retrieve a box. Unclasping a chain from around her neck, she slid a brass key off the necklace and twisted it into the lock on the box. "Here—try these." Cora flipped the lid and sprinkled a packet of tiny pebbles into my palm. They looked like seeds. I closed my fist and instantly felt a jolt of magic.

A strange sensation moved over my skin like a snake coiling around my arm. Then, at the base of my wrist, the first dark line appeared. They multiplied, creating a tattoo of twisting vines. When they reached my elbow, they stopped.

I opened my fist, and the seeds looked shrunken and withered. Releasing them from my grip, they bounced against the counter.

"What's happening to your arm?" Bowen reached for me, but I ducked out of his grasp.

"Don't touch me, just watch."

"Liana..." Bowen's tone was wary, but he kept his distance. He looked as if he wanted to call the whole thing off, willing to forgo the test the second it appeared to cause me harm.

Pacing a few steps toward a dingy window, I located a ceramic planter resting on a stone slab. Inside was a wilted fern, its leaves brown and dry. I dug my fingers into the dirt, knuckles deep, and hissed in a breath as the magic flared under my skin. The dark lines swirled slowly down my arm, receding past my wrist and over the back of my hand.

As the magic drained from my arm and into the dirt, the fern sprouted new leaves. Lush and thick, the plant grew toward the ceiling. The scent of fresh foliage filled the shop.

"Whoa... She's the real thing," Cora said, her voice

barely more than a whisper.

I removed my hand, shaking away the last dregs of magic that tingled in my fingertips. It took a moment for the pins and needles to fade, but I glanced up at the towering fern with a feeling of pride.

"That's how moving a source of magic from one place to another is supposed to work." I fixed Cora with a sarcastic smile. "Assuming you have a proper source."

Bowen's gaze found mine, and I experienced a strange flutter in my chest. He was impressed. Crossing to the window, he took my arm and traced the path the vines had made with his fingers. His touch created a little sizzle across my skin that had nothing to do with any lingering magic.

"Does it hurt when you do that?" he asked.

"It depends. Plant magic kind of tickles."

"Are you satisfied now, Cora?" Bowen squeezed my hand and led me back to the counter.

Cora sniffed the air and took out her ledger, flipping to an empty page. "What are you looking to purchase?"

"Blue flame crystals," I said, watching as she made a notation in her log.

"It will take me a couple of days, but it shouldn't be a problem. I'll let you know when they're in stock."

"Pleasure doing business with you." I winked, and her nose twitched in an effort to contain a snarl. Bowen offered her a small pouch of coins, promising the rest of her fee once the crystals arrived.

We left the shop and made our way back down

the staircase. I could barely contain my laughter as I stepped out into the alley.

"Did you see her face when that fern shot to the ceiling? I thought she was going to lose it."

Bowen chuckled. "Cora doesn't like to be proven wrong. You're lucky she gave you a packet of seeds on the second try. That woman's vengeful."

"Well, so am I."

"Don't I know it." He grinned and went to untie the horses, but I placed a hand on his arm, stalling him. It felt good to be back in my old stomping ground, and I wasn't ready to leave yet.

"You know," I hedged, "as the winner in our duel yesterday, you haven't asked me yet what I want as my prize."

"Your prize?" He almost choked on the question.

"Well, yeah. To the winner goes the spoils. And I won fair and square."

"That's debatable." He scrubbed a hand over his face, glancing around the empty alley. "What did you have in mind? I'm a busy man. I have a—"

"Yes, I know, you have a schedule to keep. Whatever that means. I have yet to witness this elusive schedule. Buy me a drink in the tavern at the end of the street."

"Liana...no. I don't go to those types of public places."

"Why not?" I sputtered. "You're practically a legend. You know, they tell stories about you around the firepit in my village. That's what I want. I want to hear one of your stories in a tavern, holding a mug of ale, like a normal person."

His eyebrows drew together in a quizzical look. Probably from my use of the term "normal person." As far as he was concerned, I was as normal as they come. But that couldn't be further from the truth.

An internal debate raged before he finally tugged the hood of his cloak over his head, effectively hiding his features. "One drink."

"Two."

"Don't push your luck," he grumbled, leading me down the alley toward the tavern.

Chapter 11

Liana

The tavern was more crowded than I expected. Patrons tossed back mugs of ale and picked from plates of sizzling meats. Their raucous conversation and laughter echoed into the rafters. No one paid us any attention when we entered, except for the barkeep, who seemed to recognize Bowen even with his hood hiding his features.

A look passed between them. Bowen held up two fingers, signaling our drinks, and the barkeep angled his head toward a staircase that led to a loft. With his hand at my back, Bowen guided me up the stairs into the empty loft. We took a seat at a table overlooking the tavern, and I leaned forward against the wooden rail like a spectator watching a rowdy show.

Our drinks were served, and a single lantern illuminated a spread of thinly sliced meats and cheese. I sandwiched them together and chewed thoughtfully.

"Is this what they call the best seat in the house?"

Bowen drank deeply from his mug before answering. "This is *a* seat in the house. A secluded one. You wanted a drink and a story; you didn't negotiate where we'd sit."

I rolled my eyes and picked up my mug. The scent of barley filled my nose as I sipped the ale, savoring the cold, bitter flavor coating my tongue. It was delicious. A rare treat, and one I usually had to hide from my father back home in the village.

For a while, we sat in comfortable silence, only speaking to point out when someone below tumbled out of their seat or started shouting a sea shanty over the noise in the tavern. My mug emptied and refilled, and a pleasant buzz settled in my limbs. Bowen's gaze continuously switched from studying me to his pocket watch. After my second drink, he reached into his pocket and plunked a handful of coins down on the table.

"All right, it looks as if you've had your fill. If you keep going, I'll need to carry you out of here."

I grinned at the image his words invoked, tempted to lean over the rail and snap my fingers for a third round. Except for when he'd tossed me haphazardly onto the mattress, I enjoyed the way his arms felt around me when he kept me from falling off the nightstand. It may be the ale talking, but offering to carry me out of the tavern wasn't the threat he thought it was.

He reached out to help me stand, but I swatted his hand away, swaying a little in my chair.

"No! We can't leave yet. You haven't told me anything about you. That was part of the deal. My prize, if you recall."

Bowen's features darkened, and he braced his elbows on the table. "I really don't think you deserve a prize for allowing yourself to get hurt during a fight."

I matched his stance, leaning in with a smirk. "Yeah, well, you wanted a duel; you didn't negotiate fair play."

"You're infuriating," he mumbled under his breath.

"You're infuriating," I mocked, feeling supremely triumphant in my comeback.

His eyebrows rose, and a dry laugh escaped his throat. "Are you just copying everything I say now? Two drinks and you're a parrot?"

Am I?

I deflated a little in my seat, running my finger through a little puddle of ale next to my glass. "No."

He looked incredulous, as if he couldn't believe a girl half his size was putting him through the paces. Finally, he shook his head and leaned back in his chair.

"Fine. What do you want to know?"

After muffling a hiccup with my fist, I drained the last drops of my drink and wiped my mouth with my sleeve. "Everything! Did you really explore Ezora's tomb? And what's the deal with Cora? She's awful, but I'm dying to know what she told the pirates. Not to mention, how did you get your dreaded nickname?" My mouth clamped shut on the last one, and I stared into the bottom of my mug. *What a stupid thing to bring up!*

Bowen drew in a deep breath, and his jaw tightened.

I raised my palms, horrified by my loose talk. "I'm

sorry. You don't have to answer that. I don't know what I was thinking."

"No, it's all right. It's a fair question. In fact, you deserve to know who you're dealing with. You wanted a story. I'll tell you one."

The ale churned in my stomach, making me feel mildly sick. Bowen leaned forward until the candlelight caught his features. The sounds in the tavern faded away, and I was enthralled by his somber stare. He was such a handsome man. Arresting in a way I'd never experienced. People may say his face was ruined, but they weren't looking closely enough.

"What happened?" I whispered as if someone around us might hear. Which was a silly thing to do since we were the only ones in the loft, but it felt as if he were about to confide his secrets to me, and I was reluctant to share them.

"Well, I had just returned from overseas when I heard about a job. There are certain items in my trade that are coveted by many, the kind of treasure people spend their lives searching for. This was one of those."

I clenched my hands around the base of my mug. Still keeping my voice low, I said, "Are you talking about the Incantus?"

"How did you know about that?"

"I saw it in your drawings. You did numerous sketches of the treasure chest and the Incantus medallion. They looked important and, to be honest, a little foreboding. The strange symbols made me uncomfortable."

Bowen nodded. "People have been searching for the

Incantus for centuries. It's an item of great power. I was cocky—I thought I could find it. So I took the job. My employer wasn't exactly a model citizen. His name was Robert Lennox, and he led one of the most powerful gangs in the kingdom. Not that it mattered to me. I was in it for the treasure. Besides, if I only worked for honorable clients, I'd never work."

I smiled. "Makes sense."

"The terms were pretty simple: If and when I found the Incantus, it belonged to Robert. Any other treasure in and around the object was mine, along with a significant finder's fee. I hunted the Incantus for nearly three years, gathering all the data from the searches before mine. I thought I came close a couple of times, but no luck. Until I discovered a clue."

"What kind of clue?"

"A journal filled with code hidden inside a crypt. It took forever to decipher it, but eventually, I did. My team traveled to the location in the journal, and we found the Incantus. But that wasn't all. The treasure trove contained other artifacts, many of which we took back with us. Among them was the blue flame crossbow. I planned to add it to my collection. A trophy of sorts to commemorate the find of a lifetime."

I leaned back in my chair and exhaled. "That's incredible."

Bowen's gaze took on a faraway look. "It was. Until we returned home. See, the trouble with working for criminal clients is that you can easily get caught up in their world. My team and I unloaded the

Incantus as well as the other artifacts inside Robert Lennox's warehouse and gathered back at the manor to celebrate. Hours later, it was all gone. Burned to ashes." Bowen's hand clenched into a fist, and his voice dipped. "Robert's illegitimate son Argus Ward—who, ironically, was the leader of a rival gang—set fire to the warehouse. It was an act of retaliation against Robert, and we got entangled in it.

"At the time, it wasn't clear who set the fire, and the blame fell on us since we'd just returned with the treasure. When the flames were extinguished, everything was destroyed, but there were no remnants of the treasure, and we realized it had been stolen. Robert thought I wanted the Incantus for myself. He assumed I stole it and set the fire as a decoy.

"As punishment, he blacklisted me with every client from here to the farthest kingdom. No one would hire me. I was ruined. But that wasn't enough for him. He wanted my complete devastation; physical proof of the consequences for crossing him. So he gave me these." Bowen's hand slid down the side of his face, pointing to his scars. "After that, no one would go near me. They were too frightened."

"But that's not fair!" I nearly shot out of my chair. "What about Argus? What happened to the treasure?"

"No one knows. The Incantus has never resurfaced. Robert is presumed dead, though there are rumors they never found his body, and as for Argus, that leads us to the present. He's the leader of the gang now, and that's why I wanted the Grimm's blade. Argus is searching for it, and I plan to keep it from him."

I worried my lip between my teeth, trying to wrap my head around all the details. My heart ached for Bowen, but a part of me also feared for his future. He might think he didn't have one, but I knew better than most about moving on after loss.

Ever since I arrived at the manor, I'd heard whispers of Bowen's plan. Whispers that spoke of sparking a war between him and the local criminal element. I understood his feelings of revenge and the drive to right a severe wrong, but where did it end?

"Isn't that risky? You suffered so much. What if—?"

"Stay out of it, Liana." Bowen's tone forbade any argument, and I bit my tongue to keep from pressing the issue. I didn't have a say in his future, and even though I felt a strong desire to protect him from further hurt, it wasn't my place.

"So now you know what happened. The whole truth. I'm sure the rumors are twice as bad. I just don't care anymore. All I want is for Argus to pay, and for you to complete your commission. In a small way, it will be like having what was lost returned to me."

"I understand how you feel. More than you know."

He angled his head, brow creasing the longer he stared. I could tell he was remembering my odd behavior, fear of enclosed spaces, and the panic attack in the carriage.

"Liana, I have to ask—"

I pushed back my chair and rose unsteadily to my feet. Grabbing the edge of the table, I forced a smile and flashed a handful of coins in my palm. "I'm still thirsty. How about one more drink? My treat."

"I don't think that's a good idea."

"It's a great idea!" I said with forced cheerfulness. "Wait here." Before he could argue, I stepped away from the table and hurried toward the staircase. My alcohol-buzzed brain made the steps wobble, but I took them slowly, keeping a tight grip on the handrail.

The tavern seemed fuller than before, and I weaved through the dense crowd. At the bar, I ordered our drinks and leaned back against the counter. My gaze tracked to the darkened loft. I couldn't see Bowen, but I knew he was watching.

The rush to get another drink was a poorly planned attempt at diverting his attention from the question I was sure he was about to ask. I hated that he'd shared so much of himself but I was still reluctant to let him know about my past. I just wasn't ready. He might be used to the pitiful stares and dark looks, but I didn't think I'd ever get used to them. And that was all I got once someone knew my history.

Poor Liana Archer, the girl held captive by a witch.

"That'll be four royal coins, lady."

The barkeep's gruff voice jolted me out of my thoughts. I slid the coins across the counter and collected our drinks, grabbing a mug in each hand. I was halfway to the stairs when I heard a faint sound. At first, it was only a few notes on the air, nearly masked by the crowd, but then it grew louder, closer.

The familiar tune washed over me, and I sucked in a sharp breath, recognizing the haunting strings of the song my father used to sing to Hendrik and me before bedtime. I hadn't heard it in years. Not since the last night with the witch.

The fuzz in my brain vanished, crystallizing into sharp awareness.

A man brushed past my shoulder. As we made contact, a thick haze of magic sank into my bones. It felt oily and dense, and a numbness spread through my body. The whistling faded along with the sickening sludge of magic as the man kept moving. My heart thundered in my ears, and I spun, ale sloshing from the mugs to slap against the sticky floor. I spotted him through the crowd. A mop of blond hair peeked from beneath a woolen cap. He was tall and lanky, walking with nervous energy and a slight limp.

It can't be.

I tracked his movement across the tavern and out the door. This wasn't one of my hallucinations; guilt manifesting in the face of some young boy. This was real.

Our mugs of ale landed on a nearby table, and I bolted through the patrons toward the entrance. I came to an abrupt halt when I collided with a drunken man regaling a group of sailors with a story. My hands inadvertently clamped around his arms while I tried to keep my balance.

The stranger laughed, turning his head back to the sailors. "Look what I caught, boys. Have you ever seen —" He paused as a vacant look filtered over his face. Eyes clouding, he shook his head in confusion. I jerked my hands away in horror as I felt the pulse of magic leave my palms.

"Sorry," I mumbled, darting out of his reach. But he

didn't go after me. He rubbed his temple looking at his friends as if he'd never seen them before.

My whole body trembled as I burst through the door and out into the daylight. The street teemed with people, their heads low against the bracing wind.

"Hendrik!" I shouted his name, searching the passing faces.

At the corner, a man stopped. I caught the same flash of blond hair curling around the nape of his neck. He angled his head, and his profile made my breath catch.

It was him.

"Hendrik, wait!"

He was still for another moment, then he stepped around the corner. By the time I arrived, he was gone.

Chapter 12

Liana

Papers scrawled with Bowen's design crinkled beneath my elbows as I massaged the bridge of my nose. My eyes felt grainy, and my head pounded from lack of sleep. The multitude of hanging lanterns cast a warm glow over the workshop, but even their soft light made me squint in discomfort.

I'd tossed and turned for the past few nights, unable to get the chilling tune out of my head. Hendrik's distinctive whistle followed me everywhere. After I left the tavern, Bowen had chased me out into the street and found me leaning against a building, almost in shock. He'd questioned me, but I made up some lame excuse about the walls in the tavern feeling too close and I needed fresh air. He didn't look as if he believed me, but he let it go for the time being.

Was it really Hendrik, or was it all in my head?

Being back in the kingdom walking the same streets we did when we were younger might be causing old memories to surface, but it felt different this time. I was certain it had been Hendrik, though

I wasn't sure why he'd walked away. Unless he didn't recognize me—or worse, he wanted me to know he was alive but didn't want to talk to me.

And wasn't that my greatest fear? That he might hate me? That I didn't do enough?

After a few years of searching, Sarah and Thomas had tried to help me forget and move on with my life. We'd channeled my ability into something useful, and it gave me strength. It was the right thing to do, but it didn't heal the pain because I never truly let it go.

Maybe it was time to face the truth. Bowen's story had made me realize bad things happened to people who didn't deserve it, and it was so easy to let tragedy infect our lives and make us feel as if we had nothing left. I needed to know if the man I saw was my brother, not to absolve myself of guilt—after all, the only person who could do that was me—but to make sure he was okay.

Because the truth was I couldn't shake the queasy feeling that had washed over me when we made contact. The dull thud of magic filling my veins, then spilling into the stranger as I tried to leave the tavern. My throat closed as the unspeakable thought I'd attempted to deny forced its way to the center of my mind.

What if he hadn't recognized me because he was still under the influence of the witch?

If that were the case, it made my purpose clear. I wasn't able to save him in the past, but maybe I could do something now?

I groaned and dropped my head in my hands. I

should show Bowen the same courtesy he'd shown me and tell him about my past. But there was still a part of me that wanted to hold back. It was laughable! I hadn't known him for long, and yet my conscience was berating me for not handing him my problems on a silver platter. What did I expect him to do? Release me from our bargain and drop everything to help me find my missing brother?

Worse still, why did my heart tell me he'd do exactly that?

I pressed the heel of my hand against my chest, staring absently at his meticulous drawings. He might be exactly what I needed. Bowen was good at finding things; had made a career out of it, and had a chamber full of treasure to show for it. But this was more than that. I felt connected to him in a way I'd never experienced with anyone else, and a part of me thought he might feel the same. What if we could help each other find a way out of our collective darkness?

A pair of footsteps thudded down the hall, and I straightened, smoothing the wrinkles from my dress. I pushed the hair out of my eyes and finger-combed the ends, doing my best to appear presentable. The footsteps slowed near the entrance. I pretended to work while darting glances toward the door.

Gavin poked his head into the room. He scrubbed a hand over his groggy features, going all the way through his tangled hair. "You started early this morning," he grumbled.

I sighed and shuffled a stack of drawings, fully aware of my disappointment at it being Gavin who darkened my doorway and not a certain master of the manor.

The man was pleasant enough, always appearing rumpled and put out that the sun was shining. I was surprised to learn he lived here too. Even more so to realize MacKenzie Manor seemed to be a haven for the wounded and lost.

"It's not that early. Back home, I start before dawn."

Gavin cringed. "People like you frighten me. You're always ready to get on with the day."

I shrugged and peered past him into the hallway, trying to be as subtle as possible. It didn't work.

"Don't strain your neck looking. Our esteemed employer has left the manor. He won't be back till later." He stepped into the room and leaned against the workbench, crossing his arms and his ankles. "He does that too, you know? It's kind of funny if you think about it. The two of you keep hoping each other are around the corner and then trying to hide your letdown when it's only me or the housekeeper."

I cleared my throat and frowned. "I don't do that."

Gavin chuckled. "Sure, you don't."

I heaved another sigh. At this rate, I'd blow out all the lanterns. I went back to work, tightening a clamp to the edge of the workbench. A full minute passed before I mumbled, "So where did he go?"

"Who, the gardener?"

"No."

A smile toyed at Gavin's lips. "The carriage driver?"

"Forget I asked."

"Ah, you're no fun." He pushed away from the table,

dodging a pen I tossed his way. The pen missed and skittered across the stone floor.

"Why are you here, Gavin?"

He made a face, returning to his spot by my bench. "I'm getting asked that a lot lately. Turns out, I just got word your magic supply is ready to be picked up."

"Can't it be delivered?"

Gavin scoffed. "Cora likes to hand off her merchandise in person."

Irritation shot up my spine as visions of her flirting with Bowen filtered through my mind. "I bet she does." An idea formed, taking root. It was the perfect excuse to search for my brother and keep my secret a little longer. With Gavin as my sleepwalking chaperon, he probably wouldn't even notice when I took a brief detour. Plus, it would keep Bowen out of Cora's clutches.

Win, win.

I dusted off my hands. "Well, she'll have to deal with me instead. Let's go."

"What?" Gavin's teasing grin faltered. "No way. I'm busy. I have things—"

"Then I'll go myself." I started for the door.

Gavin groaned at the ceiling. "She's trying to kill me. Fine!" His boots echoed over the stone as he chased after me. "But don't wander off, or Bowen will have my head."

***

The blue flame crystal sparkled in the candlelight. I touched the pointed end with my fingertip and felt a little zip of ice magic.

"It's perfect."

Cora made a noise in the back of her throat and put the lid back on the box. "Did you bring payment?"

I gave Gavin a side-eyed glance and angled my head while I tucked the box containing the blue flame crystal into my satchel.

"What, me?" He scowled as he fished around in his pockets. A pouch of coins landed on the counter, and he mumbled under his breath, "Bowen had better pay me back."

Cora gifted Gavin one of her devastating smiles and proceeded to slowly count the coins. He leaned forward, elbows resting on the counter, and returned a cocky grin. *Ugh, men.* This was going to be easier than I thought. I drifted toward the door, speaking over my shoulder.

"Can you finish up here, Gavin? I'm going to run into the shop at the end of the alley and pick up a new wood file."

"Sure, sure. Pick me one up too." He waved me away, whispering something to Cora that caused her to giggle.

Closing the door tightly behind me, I made my way back into the alley and braced myself against the chill. No one else was around, so I headed for the tavern. The streets were less crowded because of the early hour, but a slimy pull of unease still knotted my stomach. I pressed forward, looking into each face that passed before entering the pub.

The barkeep looked up from drying a glass. He

watched while I approached and set the glass on the counter.

"What'll it be, lady?"

My fingers tugged nervously at the ends of my cloak. "I just need some information."

He poured me a mug of ale and swiped the foam from the rim. "Information comes with a purchase. That'll be two royal coins."

I slid the coins across the counter and pulled the ale closer, using the cool glass to steady my hands.

"I'm looking for a man I saw here a few days ago. He was tall, thin, wore a dark coat and brown cap."

"Sounds like every man in here, lady." The barkeep frowned and began drying another glass.

"I realize that. He had blond, curly hair. I only glimpsed his profile, but he had a straight nose, narrow face..." I gripped the glass tighter. My description wasn't doing much good. "Oh, and he walked with a slight limp."

"Sorry, that ain't much to go on."

"No, I suppose not." I drummed my fingers on the counter. "Oh, he was whistling too."

The barkeep flipped his rag over his shoulder and fixed me with an incredulous look. "Lady, you're in the Crown Pub. This place is full of drunkards and wastrels. All they do is whistle and sing and make noise. Half of them walk with a limp. Now, unless he had some other distinguishing mark, take your drink and go." When I couldn't give him anything else, he shook his head and walked the length of the bar to help another customer.

I hung my head, wishing I could bang it against the wood. Did I really think I'd just walk in and find Hendrik sitting at the corner table after he'd been missing for six years? No way would it be that easy.

A disgusted laugh bubbled in my throat, and I took a deep swig of ale. I pushed the glass aside and turned my back against the counter, looking around the tavern. No one seemed to match my description, vague as it was, but my gaze snagged on a board nailed to the wall. I crossed the room, weaving around the tables to stop in front of it.

Similar to the board at the agency, it was covered with paper. Most of the listings were for odd jobs or items for sale, but the one that caught my eye was the drawing of a young boy. It was the same missing boy who had been posted at the agency.

Ethan Bauer. Age fourteen. Last known residence: Ever Haven for Orphans.

A woman made a tsking sound behind me, and I turned to find her frowning with a serving tray balanced on her hip. "It's such a shame what happened to that family."

"Did you know them?"

She nodded, angling her head to study the missing poster. "The Bauers were locals and worked in the market. Good people. The parents are gone now, died of some sickness, but the two children were relatively lucky. They were sent to the orphanage."

"Two children?"

"Yes, there was Ethan and his younger sister Annie. It's a shame he's gone missing. I hope they find him."

My mind raced. Ethan had a younger sister? It was probably a coincidence, but I couldn't shake the uneasy feeling.

"You haven't noticed a tall man with blond, curly hair and a slight limp in here lately, have you?"

"Now you mention it, there was someone here the other day, served him myself. But I didn't recognize his face and haven't seen him since. We do get a lot of people who are just passing through."

I sighed and thanked her before she moved on to serve her drinks. At least the sighting was something. But I wasn't any closer to finding Hendrik.

Looking over my shoulder to make sure no one was watching, I pulled the missing poster down and folded it in half, then I slipped it into my satchel next to the box containing the blue flame crystal. I roamed the pub a final time, walking the perimeter before returning to the street. Gavin was probably looking for me, but maybe he thought I'd stopped at a few more shops. It couldn't hurt to keep searching a little more. It might be a while before I got another chance.

Moving with the thin crowd, I stopped at the corner where I last saw the man who might be Hendrik. I closed my eyes, trying to separate sounds from the street noise, searching for that familiar tune.

Someone rocked into me, shoving me forward a step. I froze, blinking at the young man with the cap pulled low over his face. Disappointment surged in my chest when I realized it wasn't Hendrik, but the emotion turned to shock as he grabbed my arm to steady me then reached with his other hand to jerk the satchel off my shoulder. He pushed me against the building and took off, the crowd swallowing him up as he ran.

"Hey, thief! Get back here!" I chased after him, barreling my way through a crush of bystanders. I strained to keep him in sight as he rushed between a set of buildings, disappearing down an alley.

I skidded to a halt at the entrance to the alley, uncertain if I should follow. But he had the blue flame and the drawing. I couldn't let him get away with both.

Decision made, I followed him down the narrow path. The farther I went, the tighter the passage became until it felt as if the walls were closing in. Deep shadows caused my chest to ache with a familiar fear that made my vision blur and my heart pound. Panic tried to get a stranglehold, but I forced it down, determined to find the thief.

Turning down another alley, this one wider, I saw a flash of movement and stopped. Three sets of eyes turned in my direction. The men were young but rugged, their features rough from living on the streets. The group moved as one, slithering around me. Wicked smiles curled their lips as they advanced.

"Hey there, pretty lady. Do you have more treasures in your pockets? It's been a while since we've had a proper meal." The thief rifled through my satchel and held up the blue crystal to show the others. "This should fetch a nice price, but I bet you have more."

I edged backward, studying each of them one at a time. *Three against one. Not ideal, but not impossible either.* My hand slipped through the folds of my cloak, wrapping around my concealed dagger.

"Please, I don't want any trouble. Just give me back my things." My voice wavered.

The leader laughed, the sound bouncing off the dirty stone. "Too bad you already found it." He stepped forward, wrapping his hand around my arm, digging his fingers deep into my skin. I winced. His hot breath assaulted my neck as he slid close and whispered, "Let me see what else you got on you."

His meaty paw plunged into my cloak pocket, pulling out a handful of coins. As he went for the other side, I unsheathed the dagger and raised it to the thief's throat.

The man smirked in direct defiance at the razor-sharp steel pressed against his skin. "Aren't you just full of surprises?"

Behind him, the other two brandished blades of their own, their gazes darting between me and their leader, waiting for a sign.

"Give me back my things, and I'll let you leave in one piece," I said, holding the dagger steady.

The man's smug grin widened. "I don't think so. I like my chances. It's three against one, and those are good odds."

"For who?"

Laughing softly, the man flexed his fingers. "The girl's daft! She can't do simple math." He winked. "For me, sweetheart. The odds favor me." He backed up, tossing the crystal in the air and catching it as his cronies moved in. "Get her, boys, and don't worry about messing up her pretty face—she won't be needing it when we're through."

Chapter 13

Bowen

Climbing up the rocky path toward the manor, I stretched the muscles in my neck to ease the tension in my shoulders and adjusted the sketch pad beneath my arm. After overseeing the latest delivery of items for my new and improved workshop, I'd decided to spend the rest of the morning walking the grounds.

I'd taken my charcoal and sketch pad with me out of habit, with no intention of actually using it. What was the point? The spark was gone. The urge to create had withered along with the other facets of my life. Yet for the first time in years, I stood facing the ocean, wondering if the outcome of that night had been my downfall or if my downfall was a thing happening still, in real-time, simply because I let it continue.

Sharing my story with Liana had somehow made me see things in a different light, and getting to know her had ignited questions I never thought I'd have to answer.

Can I start over?

I didn't know yet, but I passed half the day seated

on a rocky ledge sketching the shoreline.

Now, as I approached the manor feeling the familiar aches in my muscles from sitting in one place for too long, I also felt rejuvenated. Maybe I'd sketch a little more in my office. To say my skill was rusty was an understatement, but it was coming back to me, and soon, I'd have a completed piece.

Something to share.

A grin broke out on my face as I bounded up the stone steps of the manor. She said she liked my drawings. Would she like this one too?

"Where have you been?" Gavin pounced on me the moment I set foot inside the door. He paced the foyer, boots scuffing over the marble. His hair stood on end as if he'd been pulling it out of frustration, and not from the usual unkempt look he maintained. "This morning, you said you were going out for a little while. That was hours ago!"

I shrugged out of my coat and thrust it into Gavin's wildly gesturing hands. "I didn't realize you were paying such close attention to my activities." Charging past him, I took the stairs two at a time, eager to get back to my work before inspiration faded.

He followed on my heels, my coat still hanging from his grip. "Well, it's never been an issue before—you hardly go anywhere. But now that all hell has broken loose, you're nowhere to be found."

I paused mid-step and looked at him. He seemed more haggard than usual, yet there was a panicked energy about him he rarely displayed.

"What did you do? Wait—never mind what you

did. How did Liana retaliate? Did she impale you with something? Set fire to your liquor-infused clothing?" I stifled a grin. Anything that had sent Gavin into such a wild state must have been amusing. I was sorry I'd missed it.

When he didn't answer, my amusement faltered, and his words sent it away altogether.

"She's missing, Bowen."

I blinked, certain I didn't hear him correctly. "Missing? Inside the manor? Have you searched all the rooms? The gallery?"

"That's not what I mean." He thrust my coat back at me, but confusion made me slow to catch it. The coat landed on the floor. I didn't bother to retrieve it, already charging down the hallway toward Liana's room.

A ball of ice settled in my stomach, freezing me from the inside out. If I didn't keep moving, I might become paralyzed like the suit of armor stationed at the end of the hall.

Her door was partially open, and I stepped inside, fully expecting to see her standing by the window. She wasn't there.

She's missing.

Gavin's words echoed in my mind. He hovered in the doorway, watching me process everything.

"Explain what happened. If she's not here, then where is she? She's not supposed to leave the estate by herself. With you here, I expected you to watch her. You had one job!"

"Yes, well, let it be known I'm not very good at it.

She decided to go into town this morning to pick up the blue flame from Cora." He lifted a hand in defense. "Before you go crazy, I went with her. Everything was fine! Until she went down the street to another shop on her own."

"And you didn't go with her?"

"I was finishing up the transaction with Cora. I may have gotten a little distracted—you know how she is—but Liana wasn't gone for more than twenty... maybe thirty minutes."

"Thirty minutes?" I scrubbed a hand over my face, letting my fingers trail over my scars. The action grounded me like it always did. "What happened next?"

"I couldn't find her. She wasn't in the woodworking shop or any of the others nearby. I called her name, combed the surrounding streets, but I didn't see her. After searching a while longer, I came back here, thinking maybe we got our paths crossed and she'd returned on her own."

I expelled a harsh breath, forcing my body to remain still and let myself think when everything inside me wanted to rage at Gavin for leaving her in such a risky situation. A young woman alone in the market district was never a good idea, and even though I'd witnessed firsthand her ability to defend herself, it didn't ease my fury.

Gavin squeezed his eyes shut and thrust his hands through his hair. "This is all my fault. She could be anywhere." His eyes burst open. "She could be in a ditch!"

My insides clenched. "She's not in a ditch. No one is ever in a ditch," I said between clenched teeth, more to convince myself than anything else.

Gavin shook his head, guilt raging over his features. "It must have happened at least once for people to always mention it. It'll be dark soon, cold. There are, like, fifty ditches between here and town."

"Then pick one, and I'll put you in it for causing this whole mess."

Gavin retrieved my coat from the floor, and I ripped it from his hands before charging back into the hallway. We needed to search for her, retrace their steps from this morning.

What if Gavin was right? What if she was hurt...or worse? Acid coated my throat. No—she was probably sipping tea inside one of the kingdom's teahouses, laughing at giving Gavin the slip and enjoying a day of freedom.

Someone pounded on the front door. The sound echoed through the house, and we both turned toward the stairs. A look of relief washed over Gavin's face, and he said aloud what I was thinking.

"See? She came back!"

The second knock nearly rattled the door's hinges. Gavin frowned, realizing it was unlikely to be Liana. He looked sheepish.

"Maybe that's just how she knocks? Wait here—I'll go see who it is."

I didn't wait, stopping off in my office to get some money and supplies. We'd search all night if we had to. I'd get the authorities involved, the whole bloody kingdom! They could stare at me all they liked so long as we found her.

Gavin returned with a look of disbelief on his face. He scratched behind his ears, hesitating to answer, while I grew impatient.

"Who was it?" I growled.

"Well, it seems you were right about one thing: Liana isn't in a ditch." He sighed. "Sad day for ditches everywhere. When will it be their turn?"

Frustration mixed with the terror rolling through me, and I clenched my fists. "Gavin, I swear—"

"It was the authorities."

The air lodged in my throat while horrifying visions swam in my head. "Where is she?"

Gavin cringed. "She's in jail."

***

"Can't say I saw that coming." Gavin trudged behind me toward the royal prison. "I guess I should have led with jail instead of ditches. Will you slow down? My head is killing me."

I picked up my pace, snarling at Gavin over my shoulder. The entrance to the prison was a little farther ahead, and I couldn't get the image of Liana locked away in some dark cell out of my mind.

"Start thinking about which weapon you'd like me to use. My collection is vast, and I'm going to kill you with a piece of it for letting her end up in this place."

"Now, Bowen, it isn't totally my fault she's in jail. That's on her."

I turned and grabbed him by the jacket collar.

His feet scrambled for purchase on the slippery cobblestones. "It's on you. Pick something sharp."

"There's a spear I'm partial to. It's silver-tipped. Do I get a last meal?"

"No." Shoving him aside, I continued my march toward the prison. A guard stationed at the entrance gave me a nod and unlocked a heavy iron door. I nearly gagged from the rotten smell permeating the narrow tunnels that led toward the cellblock. Another guard stopped us before we could travel any farther.

"State your name and purpose."

"Bowen MacKenzie. I have release documents for Liana Archer." I passed him a batch of signed papers. "Where is she? They informed me at the agency she'd be released immediately and moved to a more agreeable location."

The guard shrugged and unhooked a giant key ring from his belt. "There's an issue. She's been difficult. We thought it was best to wait for you."

Another man dressed in official garb stepped from the shadows. He chuckled and elbowed his partner in the ribs.

"Difficult? You should have seen it! I wouldn't have believed it if I didn't witness it with my own eyes. She carved those bastards up. It was three against one, but when we arrived on the scene, there was only one left standing."

The first guard located the correct key, letting it hang in the air while he waited for the rest of the story.

"She caught a blow to the jaw and went down.

I was about to use my whistle and intervene when she reared up and kicked the thug right in the groin. I swear, his eyes crossed and his face turned blue. Felt the pain myself just looking at him." The officer shuddered from the memory.

Gavin whistled in appreciation. A red haze filled my vision.

"What happened next?" Gavin asked, leaning into the conversation.

"She stabbed him right in the shoulder, pinning him to the dirt while she yanked a crystal from his fist. It appears they stole it from her. We didn't know it at the time. Honestly, it looked as if she were the aggressor, so we rounded them all up and tossed them in here." The officer squinted in my direction, his eyebrows rising when he spotted my scars. "She asked for you. Wouldn't let anyone else near her. Screeched like a banshee, but it's quiet now. Been quiet for a long time."

"Unlock the door," I demanded, baring my teeth.

The guard fumbled the key into the lock, his gaze fixed on my fierce expression. Twisting the key, he pushed the door open and then handed me a different set.

"Last cell on the left."

We plunged down the narrow corridor. Torches bounced shadows off the stone, but there was plenty of dark behind the iron bars of each cell. A pair of rats scurried out of our path as we traveled the length of the cellblock.

The last cell was as black as night. Gavin pulled a

torch off the wall while I worked the lock.

"Liana, we're here to get you out." My voice sounded strange even to my ears.

She didn't answer. There wasn't any movement or sound, and the silence made everything worse.

When the door swung open, I slipped inside, going down on my knees in the dirt. Gavin held the torch high, lighting the cramped cell.

Liana had her back against the wall, knees pulled up to her chest. Her eyes were wide, almost catatonic, lips slightly trembling. A dark bruise marred her jaw, and blood dotted her clothes. She didn't meet my gaze, and I wasn't certain she knew I was there. I couldn't believe this was the same woman who'd taken on three street thugs and won. But I knew she carried a secret—one too painful to reveal—that caused her to turn inward when faced with captivity.

My hands smoothed over her shoulders, and she flinched. "Liana? It's Bowen. You're safe now. We can take you home."

She didn't respond.

I searched for a way to break through to her. What did she need? My thumb traced her jawline, and I swallowed around the tightness in my throat. She wouldn't want sympathy or pity. She would have made them think she was weak when she was the furthest thing from it.

"Hey..." I crouched closer, cupping her face with my palms and bringing her vacant gaze up to mine. "I heard you thrashed those men. I bet they didn't see it coming. Did you pretend to be scared? Make them think they'd win, just like you did with me? I didn't stand a chance, and neither did they."

Her eyes closed in a slow blink, which seemed like a response.

I whispered for her ears alone, "I'm so damn proud of you. They deserved it, and you showed them—hell, you showed everyone in this prison how strong you are."

An airless moment passed, and then she shivered, her hands coming up to twist in the fabric of my shirt. Liana surged forward, wrapping her arms around my neck, holding tight as another shudder rocked her slight frame.

"Bowen? You came." She whispered my name, and I closed my eyes in relief. My fingers sifted through her hair until she relaxed against me. "Those men tried to steal the blue flame. I couldn't let them get away. But then the authorities brought me here and wouldn't let me go. I thought...I thought I'd failed again."

I had to bite my tongue to keep from telling her the magic crystal wasn't worth it and she should have let it go. It was the truth, but to her, it was life or death. And that was the root of the problem. She'd risked her life to keep up her end of the contract. The bargain I'd wrung from her had gone further than I imagined, and it was wrong.

As much as I hated it, I knew what I had to do.

"You didn't fail, and they didn't get away with anything." I waved my hand around the moldy cell. "And this place? To be honest, if there were curtains, you would have had them in tatters on the floor.

That's probably why they don't put them up. People like you would keep tearing them down."

A laugh burst from her throat, and she leaned back, swiping at her cheeks. She winced when her fingers brushed the edge of her jaw, and I captured her hand between mine.

"Careful—you got a bit of a war wound there."

"You should see the other three. They need stitches." She slowly climbed to her feet, noticing Gavin for the first time. He gave her an encouraging nod. "Thank you both for coming to get me."

"This shouldn't have happened." My voice sounded hoarse. "This never would have happened if I hadn't forced you into our bargain. You should be back in your village with your family. Not here, living in some dreary manor." I took a breath, hating my next words. "I think it's time for you to go home."

Her fingers wrapped around my forearm. "But we have a contract."

"Not anymore."

She shook her head, and her lips parted in denial. "No—you don't understand. I won't go." Her gaze found mine, raw and pleading. "I can't go."

Then don't.

My glimmer of remorse had its limits, and it was crumbling fast. "Too bad. I'm setting you free. Consider your father's debt paid." I tugged my arm from her grasp and walked out of the cell.

She followed instantly, as if pulled by a string taut between us. "You can clear my father's debt, but you can't clear mine."

I paused, confusion knotting my brow. "What does that mean?"

She straightened her shoulders, determination on full display. "I haven't been completely honest with you about my past." Hesitating, she cast a wary glance at Gavin. "The truth is I used Gavin today to take me into town. I planned to slip away on purpose."

Gavin made a grunting sound and mumbled, "I told you this was her fault. Blaming me, the innocent victim, just minding my own business. He threatened me with a spear, you know? A spear! I mean, I wasn't worried, but—"

We both turned, shooting him twin glares.

His lips flattened. "Jeez—sorry. Please, continue with your deceitful confession."

Liana stepped closer and placed her hand on my arm again. This time, I didn't pull away.

"I want a new contract. One where the commission you asked for pays for something else. I need your help, Bowen. It won't be easy, and a part of me feels guilty for dragging you into my mess, but I'm asking anyway. So what do you say?"

Gavin scoffed. "That's it? He's supposed to decide based on that vague request? Bowen—"

"Shut up, Gavin." My hand closed over hers. I lifted it, entwining our fingers. "Where do I sign?"

Chapter 14

Liana

After a hot meal and a long bath, I almost felt like myself again. I'd washed away the grime and blood, and outwardly, minus the throbbing bruise on my jaw, you'd never know I'd taken on three street thugs and spent the afternoon in prison.

Inwardly though? I was ashamed to admit it, but I could still feel that clawing sense of panic as the cell door closed. The snick of the key in the lock. Darkness so thick you couldn't see the hand in front of your face. It brought everything rushing back, and I was that young girl again, trapped with no way out.

I hated those feelings! I hated the label of the broken girl, born out of tragedy and never fully rising above it. But there wasn't pity in Bowen's eyes when he opened the cell door and sank to my level. His hushed tones had said the words I needed to hear.

He was proud of me.

I hadn't failed.

The darkness had lifted along with the panic and despair. At that moment, I knew I should trust him with my secret, though it shocked me when he tried to send me away.

Maybe I should have accepted his offer to return home. With Sarah and Thomas's help, we could have searched for Hendrik again. Everything could have gone back to the way it was before.

So why didn't I jump at the chance?

You know why.

A flush spread across my cheeks. Yes, I wanted his help to find my brother, but it was more than that. We had a connection I wanted to explore. He wasn't like any other man I knew. I felt different around him; whole. As if I could say or do anything without judgment or pity.

I paced slowly in front of his office door, slippers shushing over the carpet. He'd been patient, only asking me to come down when I was ready. But now, I was too nervous to knock.

Get a hold of yourself! You're not some smitten schoolgirl. You're a grown woman who carries a dagger. Act like it. I blew out a breath, bouncing on the balls of my feet. A couple of lunges and a fake sword thrust later, I rapped my knuckles against the door.

"Enter."

The door creaked open to reveal pools of orange light. Pillar candles were perched on almost every surface, illuminating the room as I'd never seen it before. A fire burned in the hearth, and the scent of pine mingled with the faint aroma of melting wax. My first thought was how cozy it was, which was a strange description for a room containing a collection of deadly weapons.

Bowen sat at his desk, head bent over a drawing pad. His hand made quick work across the page, leaving streaks of charcoal in its wake. The light played over his intense features, accentuating the hard line of his jaw and rugged cheekbones.

My gaze dropped to his hand, captured by the way the charcoal moved in smooth strokes. He drew as if it were a choreographed act, knowing exactly where to place the charcoal. Light in some areas, dark in others. It was mesmerizing.

He ignored me until I came closer, traveling across the carpet on my own. The absence of his gaze made it easier, almost as if he were shifting the power, allowing me to advance without notice. The air seemed to thicken with each step I took. Awareness of him was a living thing now, and it touched all my senses.

I stopped at the edge of the desk and watched as his hand stilled. Charcoal smudged his fingers, and he rubbed them against a rag.

"How are you feeling?" he asked, still averting his eyes to his drawing.

"Better, thank you. Good as new." My words faltered as his gaze snapped to mine.

He scrutinized my features. I'd looked in a mirror before coming down; I knew what he saw. The ugly purple bruise marred the side of my face. Self-conscious, I pulled the thick, still-drying strands of my hair forward. I dropped my gaze to the floor as heat filled my cheeks.

Bowen shifted his weight, rising from his chair. He came around the desk, and the tops of his shoes filled my vision. Lifting my chin with his fingers, he placed an icy pouch against my jaw. I flinched in surprise, welcoming the coldness that seeped through the fabric.

He held it there until my hand covered his, then he pulled away and leaned back against the desk. "The first two melted while I waited for you to come down."

I smiled, moving the ice pack lower. "It looks worse than it is."

"You say that a lot. I'm not sure I believe you anymore."

The snap and crack of the hearth filled a long moment of silence.

"What are you drawing?" I angled my head, trying to see around Bowen's large frame.

He pulled the parchment forward, blowing charcoal dust from the surface. "It's nothing. Earlier today, I took a walk along the shoreline. Something about it must have captured my interest."

I slipped the drawing from his hands, studying the intricate detail of the cove. The surf crested over the sand, and sea spray crashed against the rocks, shooting high into the air. It was a beautiful drawing, illustrating the untamed nature of the ocean and the remoteness of the sandy coastline.

"I haven't seen you do a landscape. All the others are items from your collection or treasures you've come across. I like this one a lot."

"It's not finished," he said, placing the drawing

back on the desk.

"Yeah," I whispered softly. "Sometimes it feels as if nothing ever is." I took a breath, stalling for a moment before I continued. "I haven't been completely truthful with you about my past."

"You mentioned that."

I lowered the ice pack to my side, searching for the right words, but Bowen reached forward and replaced it against my cheek. The rough pads of his fingers cupped the back of my neck.

"You don't need to explain why you didn't tell me. We all keep secrets." An emotion flickered across his features, but it faded before I could place it. "Just tell me why you're still here."

Straight to the point. He wasn't interested in dancing around motives, and his directness put me at ease.

"The truth is, my brother Hendrik is missing. Presumed dead, actually. It's been six years since I last saw him, but a few days ago, he was in the tavern with us. I heard his voice, the song he used to whistle to calm me down. No one else knows that tune."

Bowen's brow creased. "So that's why you ran out of the pub as if a ghost were chasing you?"

I nodded. The ice pack had lost its effectiveness, so I placed it on the desk and then leaned back, mimicking Bowen's stance. Our shoulders were side by side, arms pressed together.

"What happened to him?" Bowen asked.

I ground my toe into the floor and swallowed around the lump in my throat. "It's a long story."

His shoulder bumped mine. "Aren't they all? Tell me."

Tell me a story.

My mind flashed back to my stepbrother and stepsister demanding I finish their bedtime story. Except the unhappy ending was my life and not a made-up fairy tale.

"Well, it all started with a witch. Hendrik was sixteen when he was taken, and I was fifteen." I glanced up to catch Bowen's reaction, but his features were cast in shadow. "I don't remember my mother, but my father was a wonderful man. He'd tuck us in at night when we were kids and sing a tune he'd made just for us. But over the years, we fell on hard times, and when he left to find work in the mines, he never came home.

"Without any money, Hendrik and I were forced onto the streets. For a while, things were okay. Hendrik found work, and he took care of me. But it was short-lived when he injured his leg in an accident."

"What happened next? How did you meet the witch?"

"It was my fault. I used to sell merchandise in the market, and one day, an old woman approached my stall. She seemed to know so much about us. She asked bizarre questions and even knew about the strange birthmark on my arm. Every day, she'd come back, and then she took pity on us when Hendrik lost his job. She offered us work and a place to stay. She didn't care about his injury so long as he could stack wood and feed the animals, and I could clean and do some cooking.

"I thought we were saved, and with few choices, we followed her into the woods."

"The woods?"

"Yes. She kept saying her house was just a little farther until we'd walked miles. But there it was: a cabin in the woods. She invited us in, clucked over the dirt on our faces and empty bellies. She was so gentle, her voice so soothing, that Hendrik and I both fell under her spell. After dinner, she smiled an odd sort of smile and placed a piece of hard candy into each of our empty bowls. The taste of mint is the last thing I remember."

Bowen frowned. "She drugged you?"

"Hendrik and I woke up in separate cells. Days passed, weeks maybe? The candy kept us groggy and sluggish. It was so dark…and hot. I remember the heat baking my skin."

"What did she want?"

"We didn't know. At least, not right away. It wasn't until after I developed a plan of escape that I found out what she was truly after. I waited until she delivered our food and then took her by surprise. I'd almost made it out of the cell when she grabbed me. The second she touched my arm, I felt intense pain. I had absorbed some of her magic.

"She locked me back inside, but unknowingly, I transferred her power into a wooden spoon, creating a key. We tried to get out of the house, but she caught us. Hendrik pushed me out of the way and told me to run.

That was the last time I saw him."

"And the Archers—they're not your true parents?"

"No. They found me in the woods and took me back to their village. They adopted me, gave me a new home and a new family. I don't think I'll ever be able to repay their kindness."

Bowen pushed away from the desk and turned to face me. "That's not true. You took Thomas's punishment without hesitation. You could have refused my deal and left him in prison. Most young women wouldn't have bargained with their life. You've shown incredible bravery."

I sent him a half-smile. "And yet most young women aren't afraid of the dark."

He framed my face with his hands. "You're not afraid of it. You just know what can lurk there. Not everyone sees the kind of evil you saw."

Holding his gaze, I said, "You agreed to help me. Will you go back on your word?"

Bowen's thumb ghosted over the injury on my jaw, and his gaze darkened. "My word is good. I'm assuming you want me to help you find your brother, to see if he's still alive?"

I nodded slowly. "And there's one other thing."

He lifted a brow, waiting for my condition.

"When I find Hendrik, if he's still under the witch's control, I'm going to rescue him and make sure she never hurts anyone else again."

"That doesn't surprise me."

"It shouldn't since you're wrapped up in some sort of revenge plot of your own. But I'm doing this with or without you. I just hope it's with you."

"You drive a hard bargain."

I reached into my pocket and withdrew the missing person poster I stole from the tavern. Flattening the crinkled edges, I placed it on the desk.

"This boy is missing too. He's almost the same age as Hendrik was, and he has a younger sister still at the orphanage. I don't have proof it's related, only a gut feeling, but I think we should start with this."

Bowen examined the image. "Trying to find missing people, hunting witches…it's dangerous. You could get hurt, maybe killed."

"It's possible, and if you help me, so could you."

"There's that. You said yourself I have my own plan in the works. My death would throw a wrench in it."

"Then don't die."

He grinned, and a spark flared to life behind his eyes. "Same goes for you."

I held out my hand. "Do we have a deal?"

He eyed my palm, not accepting the handshake. My fingers closed into a loose fist. Disappointment bloomed inside my chest. Was he already having second thoughts?

Something wicked flashed across Bowen's features. I held my breath as he leaned forward and brushed his hand against my waist, guiding me closer.

"Really, Liana? A handshake? That's not how you seal a deal with death on the line."

A tiny shiver raced across my skin. "It's not?"

"No." His gaze dropped to my mouth, and I reflexively bit the side of my lip. The action made his grip tighten, fingers digging into my skin. A handshake seemed ludicrous when I thought about what I wished he'd do instead.

But this was my offer, and he was asking me to give it.

There was a pang around my heart when I thought about how alone he'd been over the past few years—scorned by society, labeled a monster. I wished I could undo all the pain for him. Of course, that wasn't how tragedy worked. You couldn't erase bad memories, but you could make new ones. Better ones.

I slid my palm up the wall of his chest, smoothing my fingers over the exposed skin of his collarbone. His scars were rough against my hand. I didn't mind them, exploring their texture as my fingers curled around the back of his neck.

"Well, if a handshake won't seal the deal, how about this?" Heart-slamming against my chest, I brushed my mouth against his.

He reacted instantly, approval rumbling in the back of his throat. His palm splayed across my back, drawing me flush against his chest, and his head dipped, allowing our kiss to deepen. A shiver ran through my body as he skillfully teased my lips. This was the fearless adventurer who'd experienced life on a grand scale, and yet I tasted darkness too. I wondered if he could taste it on me.

"So is that a yes?" I breathed, arching my neck as his lips trailed along my jaw, skimming my ear.

He reclaimed my mouth as if in answer. Heat inflamed my skin as he softened the kiss, slowing the moment down until it was seared into memory.

The day we met, our handshake had been nothing more than a term of agreement, but somehow, everything had changed, and now, our kiss felt like a promise.

Pulling back, he cupped the side of my face, and the tone of his voice moved something inside of me. "Yes, I'll help you, but not for payment. Not even because it's the right thing to do."

"Then why?"

"Because you asked. All you ever have to do is ask."

Chapter 15

Bowen

Fingers snapped in front of my face, and I blinked. Gavin's familiar features came into focus.

How disappointing.

I massaged my temples, trying to recall what we were talking about before I wound up staring into space, replaying the night before for the hundredth time. How was I expected to concentrate on anything when my mind kept remembering in vivid detail the way Liana had felt pressed against my body? Or the way her mouth had fit against mine?

It was damn near impossible to hold a normal conversation.

Gavin snorted and scooped a forkful of eggs into his mouth, speaking between bites. "Are you crazy? You're hunting witches now?"

Oh, yeah, that's right. Witch-hunting.

He shook his head, chasing his meal with a glass of juice. "Do you hear yourself? Who says something like that at the breakfast table? It's not even a decent hour." He scraped his plate, the fork tines clinking against the porcelain.

I picked up the knife resting on my napkin. Gavin paused mid-scrape and eyed the serrated edge, aware of the fact my plate was empty and uses for the sharp utensil had dropped to one.

"Remind me again who lets a young woman traipse around the market district alone, putting her in a position to get mugged and thrown into jail?"

Gavin punctured the air with his fork. "Liana stabbed someone. Sure, the thief had it coming, but I maintain the jail part was on her. Besides,"—he poured himself another glass of juice—"I'd say it all worked out in your favor. You got the girl, didn't you? Though now you're talking nonsense about hunting witches, I'm having regrets about cheering you on. Regrets, Bowen! And you know I have my fair share of those." His gaze dropped to a single link of sausage remaining on his plate. Carefully, he reached out to pluck the knife from my fingers and began cutting the sausage into smaller chunks. "You weren't really going to use this on me, were you? After everything we've been through. All I've sacrificed."

It was my turn to snort. "Sacrificed? You live here rent-free, eat my food, drink my liquor—and you meddle."

Gavin conceded, nodding his head at each of my points. "Meddling is one of my numerous talents. I'll have you know, our dagger-wielding friend has been quite put out every time I showed up in her workshop when she was expecting you. Not that I relish a woman's disappointment at seeing my face. It certainly has never happened before, but I admit, I've started doing it on purpose." He leaned back in his chair and grinned. "I stole a pair of your shoes once and tried matching your hulking gate. I even wore one of your coats. Fooled her good that time."

"You have too much time on your hands." I scratched the back of my neck, oddly flattered by the thought Liana might have been hoping to see me. Not that I would admit it to Gavin. "I'm sure her disappointment had more to do with enduring your dreary personality than the lack of my presence."

"You're talking nonsense again. Nothing about me is dreary." He rose from his chair and attacked the sideboard, refilling his plate with second helpings.

I eyed the door to the dining room, wondering how much longer I should wait. Was she coming down to breakfast?

Last night was a revelation in more ways than one. I may never be able to heal the scars on my face, but I could help the scars of her past fade. There was so much evil in the world and no end to how it altered people's lives.

Who would she be without the guilt, the anger, and ultimately, the fear that ruled her life? Would she still face each day with bravery? Hide her fighting skills behind a coy smile, taking pride in the fact most people underestimated her? Her past had shaped her into the woman she was today, and the devil in me was grateful.

My past had a stranglehold around my neck, but for the first time, I wondered if it had shaped me in a way I didn't expect. What if it had molded me not into a bitter man driven for revenge, but into a man destined to rise from the ashes for the sake of another?

Gavin must have read my thoughts. He folded his arms across his chest, and his eternal grin vanished from his features.

"Since you've decided to go all witch-hunter on me, what are you going to do about Argus and the Grimm's blade? Don't tell me your lust for revenge is waning because of a girl. I won't be able to keep my eggs down."

"If you lose your breakfast, it's because of your hangover this morning, not because of my actions. Besides, if I remember correctly, your situation isn't that different from mine. How does the saying go—pot meet kettle?"

Gavin's smile returned, but now, it was dry and brittle. "We aren't talking about my vices. And we certainly aren't talking about my past." He eyed the knife in his hand—the one I used as a mild threat. I'd pushed him too far. It was one thing to joke about his self-destructive habits, and entirely another to mention her—the woman who'd vanished into the sea.

My palms lifted in defense. "Fine. Back to your question. The Grimm's blade is safe for now. Argus will come for it, and I'll do what needs to be done. It's too late to turn back now."

Gavin rubbed a hand over his face and pushed aside his plate. Silence fell between us as we each wallowed in our thoughts. It wasn't until we heard commotion in the hallway that we both looked up.

Brutus barked, and his nails clicked across the floor as he neared the dining room. Jacob's awed voice echoed down the hall.

"Did you really thrash three street thugs all by yourself, Miss Archer?"

Liana's entourage preceded her into the room. Brutus sat next to the threshold, waiting for her to enter, while Jacob danced on the balls of his feet, throwing fists at imaginary villains. He thrust an uppercut into the air.

"Did you get 'em like this?"

"No, it was like this!" Liana sailed into the room, jabbing an invisible dagger into the air. Grinning from ear to ear, she twisted the hilt then wiped imaginary blood onto her skirt. She faltered when she spotted us lounging at the table.

I lifted an eyebrow, enjoying the way her cheeks blossomed pink when she realized she'd been caught pantomiming her fight.

"No weapons at the breakfast table, Jacob," she said sternly, pretending to sheathe her invisible blade.

"Yes, Miss Archer." Jacob stifled a smile and picked up a plate.

"Good morning, Liana." I smiled and poured her a cup of coffee. She accepted the steaming cup and brought it to her lips, taking a contented sip.

"Good morning, Bowen." She held my gaze over the brim of the cup.

Gavin made a disgusted sound and tossed his

napkin onto his plate. "What am I, day-old bread? And this after I woke up early just to see how you were feeling."

Liana lowered her coffee. "Good morning to you too, Gavin."

"Save it. He's all yours. Go hunt witches to your heart's content. I'll be in my room, doing what I do best: napping." He rose from his chair and walked toward the door, patting his thigh to get Brutus to follow.

The dog didn't budge.

"Traitor dog. Switching sides because of a pretty girl. That seems to be running rampant in this house," he grumbled, his voice carrying down the hall.

Liana's gaze darted back to mine, and I tensed at her reaction to Gavin's statement. "Is what he said true?"

I opened my mouth to answer and paused, feeling a tingling sensation at the back of my neck. Her blush must have been catchy because I felt heat rise under my skin. "Gavin isn't lucid on his best day. He doesn't know what he's talking about." I winced at the gravel in my voice.

"Lucid or not, you told him about our plans."

"Oh." I coughed into my hand. "You meant the witch. Gavin's trustworthy, and I didn't tell him everything."

She narrowed her gaze and crossed her arms, the universal signal for "tell me the truth."

Why is it so bloody hot in here? I tugged on my collar.

"Fine. I told him everything," I mumbled.

Liana sighed and cast her eyes to the ceiling. "And they say women like to gossip. The two of you are giving them a run for their money."

"Did you say something about a witch?" Jacob asked between a mouthful of toast.

"Take your plate and run along, Jacob. You have your chores and then training." I leveled him with an authoritative "don't ask questions" look, which deflated his enthusiasm.

Liana turned her attention to my plate. "You haven't eaten?"

"I waited for you," I muttered, pushing back my chair and heading toward the line of food chafers. Steam rose from the serving dish of eggs and sausage. I scooped a pile onto my plate.

Liana brushed her arm against mine, reaching over me to grab a piece of toast. The serving spoon banged against the dish, and the corner of her mouth curved at my obvious tension.

"Do you want to *switch sides?*" There was a teasing quality to her voice that made my hand still. She had heard Gavin's parting remark and decided to use it against me.

Perfect.

I rested the spoon on the edge of the dish and caught her eye. A spark of challenge lurked in her gaze. Without answering, I took a small step backward. My hands slid over her shoulders as she moved in front of me, our bodies fitting together. She didn't take the final step to the right and instead dropped her head back until it rested under my chin.

"Did you sleep well? How's your jaw this morning?" I asked, my breath wisping the hair on the top of her head.

"I slept like the dead, and my jaw hurts. What about you?"

Usually, I tossed and turned, plagued with insomnia, but not last night. I lowered my head, breathing in her scent. She smelled like vanilla and coffee.

"I slept—"

The crash of Jacob's plate cut off my answer.

"Brutus, no! Sit," the boy scolded the dog.

Liana straightened and slid past me, our places switched. She busied herself with heaping food onto her plate. A smile trembled at her lips as Brutus tried to scoff down Jacob's meal.

"Both of you, out!" I commanded, pointing toward the door.

Brutus whined, licking his lips, looking wounded. Jacob huffed and tried to salvage the rest of his breakfast. He snapped his fingers, and Brutus followed him from the room.

"So many interruptions," I grumbled, placing my plate on the table. "I can't get any peace and quiet." I pulled out Liana's chair, and she slipped into the seat, unfolding a napkin across her lap.

She shook her head and speared a sausage link with her fork. "You know, for someone who complains about the noise as much as you do, you seem to surround yourself with an excessive amount of chaos."

"What are you saying?"

"I'm saying you actually enjoy it, and you'd miss it if it went away. Frankly, you make a terrible recluse."

I almost choked on my eggs and pounded on my chest to clear my throat. "I am not a terrible recluse."

"Oh, really? So you're not planning on joining me today for a visit to the orphanage, which will be filled to the rafters with chaos-inducing little children?"

She had me there. I made a face, intending to change the subject before she made me admit she was right. Reaching across the table, I grabbed my sketchbook and opened to a blank page.

"The drawing of Ethan you showed me last night gave me an idea. What if we made one of Hendrik? As siblings, the two of you will share some common family features, and based off your description from when he was younger, as well as the man you saw in the tavern, I should be able to do an age progression that could come close."

Her breath caught, and she paused mid-bite. "Can you really do that?"

"It can't hurt to try. People respond better to images. It triggers their memory in a way a verbal description won't. We can have them mass-produced. I'm sure someone at the Gazette owes me a favor for practically selling their papers for them every time I returned from an expedition."

Liana blinked, and tears welled in her eyes. She swiped them away. "I swear I'm not crying, but yes, please. Tell me what I have to do."

"It's pretty simple. Start by describing Hendrik

when he was a teenager. That's your strongest memory of him. I'll get a baseline, and then we'll layer in the description from the tavern as well as match some of your adult features."

"All right, sounds easy enough."

"Just take your time."

She nodded, closing her eyes and starting with the distinct shape of his face, the curvature of his jawline, and the composition of his facial characteristics. She described the thickness of his brow, the way his nose turned up slightly at the end, and the narrow line of his mouth.

I sketched lightly, taking into account the adjustments as she moved on to the description of his face from the tavern. She noted the blond hair that had a tendency to curl and the way it had framed his ears.

When she finished, it was my turn to study her. She held still under my observation, afraid to even finish her breakfast if it might alter her expression.

"Your eggs are getting cold," I murmured, shading in definition with the charcoal.

"I'm too nervous to eat." She angled her head, trying to get a peek at the portrait, but I shifted, wanting to wait until the drawing was finished before I got her reaction.

Her fingers drummed impatiently against the table. "Are you finished?"

"Almost. Just a few more finishing touches." I sketched for a few more minutes before placing the charcoal down on the table. "Are you ready?"

"I think so. Wait." She shook out her hands and blew a breath. "Okay, I'm ready."

Pulling the drawing off the sketchbook, I slid it across the table. She picked it up and held it between trembling fingers.

"What do you think?" I asked.

Visibly swallowing, she pushed out of her chair, leaving the drawing beside her plate of uneaten food. She stood by the window staring out across the front yard, not saying a word.

I glanced at the sketch and frowned. Was it even close? It had to be, but I was starting to think maybe this was a bad idea. Cautiously, I joined her at the window.

"Liana, if it's not right, we can try again. Or not. It's your choice." At her continued silence, I succumbed to the urge to ramble. "I'm still pretty rusty. Any errors are from me, not your description. Maybe we could—"

She turned from the window and wrapped her arms around my waist, resting her head against my chest. "It's perfect. I never imagined…" She tilted her head back, locking her gaze with mine. A fresh wave of tears glistened in her eyes. "For someone who acts as if they have nothing left to give, you sure give a lot. Your time…your money…" She smiled. "Your talent."

Relief washed through me, and I lowered my mouth to hers, unable to believe I'd lasted the entire morning without trying to kiss her. I tasted the salt as her tears escaped and rolled down her cheeks.

"It must be because I'm a terrible recluse."

A laugh bubbled through her tears, and she

returned my kiss, then whispered, "I knew you'd eventually switch sides."

Chapter 16

Liana

With the new picture of Hendrik in hand, we made a stop at the Ever Gazette. Thanks to Bowen's connection, they agreed to print the missing poster, and one of the paperboys even offered to distribute the image around the kingdom. I couldn't believe how much progress we'd made in such a short time.

Now, we were headed to the orphanage to investigate Ethan's disappearance and check on his sister, Annie. I stared again at the young face peering back at me on the poster in my lap. The eerie similarities between us made my belief we were all connected feel stronger. Ethan's drawing made him look weary, as if he'd lived and experienced more than someone his age should. When I looked in the mirror after escaping the witch, I'd projected the same weariness. I recognized the bone-deep knowledge that I wasn't like other people and never would be.

Bowen sat quietly on the seat across from me as our carriage rumbled slowly down the cobblestone street. I was getting used to the confined space, associating it with a positive outlook. I wasn't trapped inside the carriage; it was taking me to where I wanted to go. So many things were changing, and I was changing along with them.

My mind flashed to the night before. It wasn't bravery or a sense of gratefulness that offered him a kiss. I'd wanted to feel close to him. To see if I'd only imagined the warm, fluttery feeling inside my chest whenever he was around.

I hadn't imagined it.

It only magnified at breakfast, when he'd used his talent to help find Hendrik. But in the end, the joke was on me. For a girl who'd spent most of her life not letting anyone get too close, I'd become acutely aware of just how much I wanted that to change.

"What are you thinking about?" Bowen asked.

The drawing slipped from my lap, and I made a mad dash to catch it before it hit the carriage floor. I peered up at him, mouth opening and closing without an answer. "Nothing," I mumbled.

"Your ears are red."

"No, they're not."

He grunted and tried to contain a smile. "How would you know? You can't see your ears."

I scoffed and slumped back into the seat, making sure to pull my hair forward to hide the offending appendages. Folding the drawing into my satchel, I fumbled for a safe topic of conversation—anything to divert the attention from my wayward thoughts and their desire to pick up where we left off in front of the window.

"We should probably get our story straight. They're not going to let complete strangers wander around the orphanage asking questions about missing children."

Bowen shifted to the edge of his seat. "Good point. What did you have in mind?"

Wringing my hands together, I bit the side of my lip. "I have an idea, but I'm not sure if you'll like it."

"Whatever it is, it's probably fine so long as you don't intend to hold everyone hostage with your dagger until you get answers."

I scrunched my nose. "The thought had crossed my mind, but no. I think our best advantage will be to meet with the headmistress as an interested party."

Bowen's brow creased. "An interested party? I don't follow."

Coughing lightly, I slid my gaze to the backs of my hands, hoping to get through my explanation without embarrassing myself. "Well, we are visiting an orphanage. I believe if we present ourselves as a couple looking to adopt, we may be able to tour the property and question some of the staff. They might let us visit with Annie." I looked up as I finished, hesitant to see Bowen's reaction.

"You want to pretend to be married? To me?"

"I mean...unless you have a better idea."

"No—it's just—" he stammered.

The carriage jolted to a stop in front of the orphanage, and Bowen pushed open the door and exited the carriage. I stayed in my seat, gathering the courage to follow. It was my idea after all, but now I'd put it out there, I wasn't sure how to act, and Bowen's reaction wasn't helping.

He paced outside the carriage, his boots pounding the gravel until he thrust his head back inside the carriage and offered his arm. "Let's go, wife."

I placed my hand on his arm and steeled my nerves. "Are you sure? If you'd rather the dagger idea…"

He tugged me from the carriage and tucked me against his side. "It's too late for that now. Maybe next time."

***

The headmistress studied us from over the brim of her teacup. Well, actually, she studied *me*. Every time her gaze drifted toward Bowen, it darted away. I plastered a smile on my face even though I wanted to smack her for her rudeness.

"As I was saying, Mrs. Higgins, my husband and I have recently married." I gripped Bowen's hand, finding it cold to the touch. He'd gone quiet ever since we entered the office, and I could tell he was uncomfortable by the headmistress's examination.

Mrs. Higgins set down her cup of tea. "I see, and you're interested in adopting one of our fine children? I admit, we usually cater to older couples…but I can see why you might be interested." Her gaze finally landed on Bowen's face, narrowing in on the scars. She visibly swallowed.

I bristled at her insinuation. How dare she assume his disfigurement disqualified him from having children of his own. A biting remark was on the tip of my tongue, but I held it back, lest we be thrown out. I wished more and more we'd considered the dagger idea.

"Actually, this isn't the only institution we've visited," Bowen said, removing a bag of coins from inside his jacket pocket. He placed it heavily onto the desk. "We haven't decided on where we plan to invest our time or our money."

"Of course!" Mrs. Higgins choked out, unable to tear her eyes away from the fortune gracing her desk. "Well, Ever Haven is certainly the right place for you. We have a stellar record."

I leaned forward and collected the satchel, noticing the way the headmistress's gaze followed the money. "That isn't what we've heard. It's come to our attention one of your charges has gone missing. How do you explain that?"

Mrs. Higgins fanned herself, looking slightly ill. "You've seen the posters? We're doing everything possible to find young Mr. Bauer. It's not Ever Haven's fault he's a runaway. We've had issues with him in the past. He's not representative of the other children at our institution."

A runaway? I didn't believe it for a second. Not if he had a younger sister at the orphanage as well. He wouldn't have left her behind.

"We'd like to see for ourselves if you don't mind." I leveled her with an accusatory glare and watched the color drain from her face.

"Certainly. I'll arrange for one of our staff members to show you around. I'm sure you'll be pleased with what you find. You can be confident we are the right institution to invest your money—and your care," she added as an afterthought. Rising from behind her desk, she skirted the edge and called into the hallway.

A young woman rushed into the office and dipped into a low curtsy.

"Beth, please give Lord MacKenzie and his wife a tour of the grounds and answer any questions they may have."

"We'd like to visit with some of the children as well," I added.

"Naturally."

I handed Bowen the satchel of coins, and he tucked it back inside his jacket. Mrs. Higgins almost pouted. He followed Beth from the room, but I lingered, unable to shake the anger at her judgment.

If this was the type of behavior Bowen encountered whenever he went into public, no wonder he'd closeted himself away at the manor. Maybe he'd hardened himself enough to tolerate the slights and open-mouthed stares, but I hadn't.

I picked up my steaming cup of tea and flashed her a brittle smile. "I noticed you had trouble looking my husband in the eye." Tipping the cup over, I let the tea spill onto the lightly hued carpet, staining it a dark amber color. "There—now I've given you something to stare at so you don't look like such a fool." I tossed her the empty cup, which she juggled but couldn't quite catch.

It landed with a thud next to the stain.

Mrs. Higgins sputtered as I left the room. I caught

up with Bowen in the hallway, and he shot me a questioning look.

I shrugged. "I wanted to finish my tea. It was so delicious."

Bowen leaned down and whispered near my ear, "Is she bleeding?"

A scoff burst from my lips. "What a silly question. Of course she's not bleeding. I have other sides to my personality. They're not all violent."

He didn't look as if he believed me. "You don't need to confront everyone who stares. It doesn't bother me as much as it used to."

"It bothers me," I said, knowing I'd defend him again given the chance.

Bowen shook his head as Beth strode down the hall, calling to us over her shoulder. "This way, you two! I'll introduce you to some of the children. Did you have an age and gender in mind?"

"Definitely a girl," I said. "You know, we were just speaking with your headmistress about how terrible it is that one of your charges has gone missing. And we were saddened to learn he has a younger sister here. If it's not too much trouble, we'd like to check in on her and see how the orphanage is handling her care."

"I can assure you, we provide all our charges with the highest care. You needn't worry."

I leveled her with a determined look. "We insist."

Beth nodded, but her features were pinched. "Of course. Right this way."

She led us to the second floor and down a long

corridor. Most of the rooms were massive and filled with bunk beds, housing at least twenty children at a time. A few of them peeked out the door as we walked past, whispering behind their hands. We continued down the hall, turning into another wing, where the rooms grew smaller and there weren't any other children.

Beth paused outside a door. "Annie was moved to a solitary room so she wouldn't disturb the other girls."

"Disturb them?" I asked.

"Oh, it's nothing to be overly concerned with. She likes to tell stories, but they were starting to scare the girls, so we thought it best to separate them. It's to be expected. She's started lashing out since her brother left."

"You believe he ran away?"

"Yes, I do." Beth ushered us inside the room, putting an end to further questions.

The little girl sat alone at a small table. She looked to be about six or seven. So much younger than I imagined. So much younger than I'd been.

A single window spilled sunshine across the papers scattered beneath her tiny hands. Her fingers were smudged black with charcoal. Limp brown hair hung in her eyes as she bent over her drawings, oblivious to our presence. She reminded me of a forest sprite with her pixie nose and narrow ears. There was a nervous energy about her as she used her fingers to blend the charcoal into the paper.

"Annie?" Beth stepped in front of us and gained the girl's attention. "Why don't you put your drawings away and say hello to Lord MacKenzie and his wife, Liana?"

Annie didn't lift her head but looked up with her eyes. Her blue gaze overflowed with wariness and distrust.

I was about to say hello when a bell sounded. Beth started and looked over her shoulder.

"I'm afraid I'm being summoned. If you'll follow me, we can come back later."

"If it's all right, we'd like to visit with Annie for a bit. We can stay here until you return," I said.

Beth looked uncertain and dropped her voice to a whisper. "Are you sure? Annie can be a little temperamental."

"Nonsense." I nudged Beth toward the door as the bell chimed again.

The woman shot a final glance at Annie who had resumed her drawing. She tossed up her hands in defeat, then she hurried from the room.

Once we were alone, I approached Annie slowly, keeping my actions fluid and calm. Annie followed me with her eyes, still scratching charcoal into the parchment. When the charcoal stopped, so did I.

"That's a beautiful drawing. Do you think I could try to make one too?"

Annie hesitated for a moment. Her gaze moved from Bowen then back to me. Finally, she snapped her charcoal in two and slid a clean sheet of paper across the table. I picked up the piece of charcoal she offered and knelt beside the girl. The only sounds in the room were the charcoal sticks marking the paper. Bowen hovered a few feet from the table, watching us both.

As the minutes passed, Lily grew interested in my drawing. She slowed her movements to watch mine. "Your drawing is nice too," she whispered.

"Thank you," I said, continuing to draw.

"Do you want to make one, sir?" Lily addressed Bowen with an unsure smile.

When he nodded, she snapped her charcoal again and handed over the nub.

I leaned in and said, "You're in for a treat, Annie. Bowen is a very good artist."

Bowen lowered himself to the floor, his huge frame taking up one whole side of the table. He held his piece of charcoal over the parchment and muttered, "I'm not sure how good I'll be at drawing flowers and kittens like the ones in your picture."

Annie giggled, and her entire face lit up. "That's not a kitten, sir. It's my brother."

"Oh, sorry," he mumbled, rubbing the back of his neck. He was ridiculously out of his element, but it was strangely wonderful to watch.

"What do you like to draw, sir?"

"Weapons," Bowen said.

"You do?" Annie breathed in awe. "My brother likes to draw enemies fighting, but his weapons all look like sticks. Will you draw me one so I can show him when he gets back?"

The hope in her voice was nearly my undoing. It sounded so much like the hope I'd held onto for years after I escaped the witch. Bowen must have heard it too because he smiled softly and nodded.

"Sure thing, Annie." His charcoal moved across the page, creating the outline of a sword.

"Do they hurt, sir?" Annie asked, angling her head with curiosity. She pointed to one of the scars running down Bowen's jaw.

He turned his face away slightly. "No. Not anymore."

Annie nodded, looking thoughtful. She went back to her drawing but continued to speak. "One time, I was running through the streets with my brother, and I tripped and fell on my arm. It hurt terribly. Not anymore though." Annie paused and rolled up her sleeve. "It left this mark, and sometimes when I look at it, I remember how much it hurt. Do you remember too?"

Bowen drew in a deep breath. "I remember."

"I cried and cried 'cause the mark was so ugly, but one day, my mom took my arm and kissed it. She told me she only kisses beautiful things, and that meant the mark was beautiful too. My mum got really sick and died a while back, but you know what, mister?"

"What?"

"Now, when I look at my arm, I remember her, and I kind of like it. I like yours too."

Bowen's startled gaze found mine. Time seemed to slow as dust motes, illuminated by the sun, floated in the air. I smiled, and without breaking eye contact, I added to Annie's story.

"You know, I also have a mark on my arm, and whenever I look at it, I remember someone too." My voice dipped. "And I kind of like it."

Bowen's gaze dropped to the spot he'd injured in our duel.

"Did they kiss it better like my mom did?" Annie asked.

"No, I'm afraid not."

Annie heaved a heavy sigh. "That's too bad."

"Yeah, too bad indeed."

My lips quirked, and I lifted a brow in challenge. Bowen's eyes darkened. He looked as if he wanted to make things right where my arm was concerned.

Annie, completely unaware of our little moment, held up her drawing. In the picture stood three people at the base of a forest. There was her brother, who Bowen had confused with a kitten, and also what looked like a little girl. It was the image of the woman off to the left of them that unnerved me. Annie had used deep strokes of charcoal, almost tearing through the paper, to draw the figure. Everything about the woman was dark, and I noticed while the two children were standing in the sun, the woman was almost buried in the forest.

"Who is that?" I asked, pointing to the woman in Annie's drawing.

Annie shrugged. "My brother told me about her. Sometimes, he goes to visit her in the woods. But he hasn't come back in a while. He said he'd take me with him next time."

I went rigid, holding the charcoal so tightly it dug into my palm. "Have you told anyone else about this woman?"

"Just a few of the girls. Ethan told me not to, but I

couldn't keep it a secret."

"Did your brother tell you how to find her?"

Annie shook her head, sending her brown hair swinging around her shoulders. "He's always so dirty when he comes back. The headmistress beat him because he ruined his clothes. I asked him not to go again, but he said the woman needed his help. Mine too! She gives him food, and these…" The little girl scrambled to her feet and moved toward a bed pushed against the wall. She dove underneath it, her head buried beneath the cover hanging off the side. When she came back out, she unfurled her fingers.

In her palm lay a small peppermint candy.

My breath lodged in my throat. Not only did I recognize the peppermint, but Annie had a similar birthmark to mine on her wrist.

She has the gift too.

I snatched the candy from Annie's hand. The scent of mint assailed me, and I pushed back the dark memories threatening to rush in and take over.

Bowen steadied me, concern filling his eyes. "Is that what I think it is?"

I closed my fingers around the mint, my fist shaking as I faced the truth. "It's her. The witch is back. It's happening again."

Chapter 17

Liana

"She can't stay here." I paced the hallway outside Annie's room. The candy was still clutched in my hand, and the scent of mint made my stomach roll. The last time I held one, I lost my brother, and now, that poor girl on the other side of the door might have lost hers too. "Annie has the same birthmark as me. It's not a coincidence. The witch will come after her. Bowen, she can't—"

"I know." He caught my shoulders, halting me mid-step. "I'll speak with the headmistress."

I sighed and dropped my head forward. "You didn't ask for any of this. It's too much."

"Neither did you." He lifted my chin with his thumb, holding my gaze. A wealth of emotions gathered there, and I felt lost in them.

"It will be temporary. I promise. She'll go back with me when I return home. I'd never expect..." I didn't finish the sentence. Something in Bowen's expression stopped me.

"We'll discuss that later. Wait here with Annie." His hands dropped away, and he left me standing in the hall.

Opening my hand, I stared down at the small mint. So many years had passed, and even though the memories had never left me, holding evidence of that time was like falling through a portal and landing back inside that house. The smells, the fear, the wretched heat—it all rolled over me like a thunderstorm, cracking me open and leaving me defenseless to its onslaught.

For long minutes, I was stuck inside that memory, until I heard my name, soft and inquisitive. I looked up to see Annie standing in the doorway. She twisted her hands, peering at me with uncertainty.

"Liana, are you angry with me? Did I get my brother in trouble?"

"Oh, sweetie, no." I knelt in front of her and smoothed a lock of hair from her eyes. "We're worried about you, that's all."

"You don't have to worry." A brave smile lit her features. "I can take care of myself."

It was hard to hear the words I'd said so many times. I'd taken them to heart and believed them to be true.

"I know you can. You're so brave."

She nodded, looking solemn. "My brother told me to be brave."

So did mine. A lifetime ago when he made me promise I'd run.

"I'm sure he's very proud of you." I choked on the words, hearing them spoken in Sarah Archer's calming tone. Amazingly, this time, I believed them.

I felt a presence at my back and turned to look over my shoulder. Bowen slowed his steps, watching the two of us. He nodded, answering my unspoken question.

"Thank you," I mouthed.

Annie tugged on my sleeve. "Do you want to do another drawing? It will make you feel better."

"I do, very much, but first, I need to ask you something."

The little girl angled her head and waited. I fumbled for the right words, trying to remember what Sarah and Thomas had said to me years ago when they offered to take me in. Everything back then was a blur, but something had felt right. There was a connection, a true understanding, that made me feel like a welcome addition to their family instead of a hardship.

I never really understood what they'd taken on; I was always too immersed in my own pain. But I realized it now. This promise between myself and another person to be whatever they needed me to be; to replace what they'd lost or maybe never had. It was humbling.

A flicker of impatience crossed Annie's face, and Bowen chuckled behind me. Annie tapped her foot, the sound echoing down the hall.

"She's waiting, wife."

I breathed deeply, channeling my composure. "I can see that, *dear*. I'm trying to find the right words. It's important."

His hand rested on my shoulder as he sank down

next to me. "Words don't seem to be your strong suit. You're more of a doer."

He was right.

Holding out my hand, palm up, I exhaled the nerves from my body. "Annie, if it's all right with you, we want you to come and live with us."

She eyed my hand, warily chewing on her bottom lip. "For a little while, or for good?"

I smiled. "For good."

"What about my brother? I can't leave him behind."

Her words rang in my head. So many echoes from the past.

"He'll come too once he returns. I promise."

There was only a slight hesitation before she bypassed my hand and threw her tiny frame into my arms. I rocked back on my heels, holding her tightly. Bowen squeezed my shoulder, then he rested a hand on the top of Annie's head, ruffling her hair.

"I leave with one and return with two." There was awe in his voice and a thickness that tugged at my heart.

"Go pack." I nudged Annie toward her room, hastily wiping at the wetness that clung to my cheeks.

Annie grinned and almost tripped over her feet in her haste.

Bowen held out his hand and tugged me to a standing position. I shook my head.

"How did you do it? We aren't even really married. What if they ask for proof?"

An odd expression filtered over his face. "Obviously, you didn't fully read the contract you signed when you entered my house. You should always read the fine print, wife."

My mouth dropped open. "You're not serious?" I sputtered. Mind racing, my shock slowly morphed into something else. A warm feeling spread through my chest. This was crazy, but...

Bowen's grin faltered when he noticed my expression. I heard him growl in the back of his throat. He almost sounded pained. "I was joking! But damn it, that look." His hand came up, cupping the side of my face. We stepped back in unison until I bumped the wall. "Don't look at me like that and expect me to stay still."

Every nerve in my body hummed as he pressed himself closer.

"What look?" I licked my dry lips, coming dangerously close to forgetting where we were. He dipped his head, breath fanning my cheeks and sending heat to my belly.

"The look that said you wouldn't run if it were true."

I swallowed, finding my throat as dry as my lips. My thoughts scattered as his fingers flexed over my jaw—not with aggression, but with possessive intent. For a long moment, he remained still, our breaths mingling, each of us seeing the line in the sand and wondering whether to cross.

He cursed and stepped back, spiking a hand through his hair. Muttering under his breath, he leaned against the opposite wall and watched me with conflict in his eyes.

"Money talks, Liana. It's more persuasive than a piece of paper." He paused, his voice dropping low. "And I would never trick you into something like that. You would know what you were getting into. Every last detail."

I nodded, unsure of my ability to construct an adequate sentence. In a matter of minutes, I'd been completely upended, making promises to a little girl and then secretly wishing for promises from someone else. Looking down at the floor, I pretended I could still see that imaginary line. I had stepped right to the edge. It would take nothing to cross it, and I was starting to believe it was only a matter of time.

Annie's shuffling footsteps sounded in the doorway, and we both turned to find her with a bag slung over her shoulder. It hung near her side, practically empty. She exuded hope and a dose of caution, as if she were waiting for us to change our minds. When I held out my hand again, she looked relieved.

"Ready to go, sweetheart?"

She shifted from foot to foot then withdrew a folded piece of paper and held it out to me. Charcoal splashed across the page in hasty strokes, signaling she'd only just finished. The image staring back at me made my throat tight.

A little girl stood on top of a hill with three people standing beside her. Her brother and two adults. One with long blonde hair, and the other big and tall with a scar running down the side of his face.

I looked a Bowen, and he smiled.

***

"Is this really your home, sir?" Annie whispered in awe, looking up at the towering manor from the carriage window.

Bowen followed her gaze and frowned. "It's not as scary as it looks."

"Oh, no, it's lovely. Do you play hide-and-seek in there? I bet there are tons of places to hide. Can we play?"

I stifled a laugh, trying to imagine Bowen curled up inside a cupboard while Annie counted to one hundred. He must have read my thoughts because he narrowed his eyes and crossed both arms over his chest before answering her question.

"Maybe later. After you're settled. You need time to find some good hiding places first."

Annie nodded reverently. "Good idea, sir."

"You can call me Bowen," he grumbled.

Starry-eyed, she nearly bounced in her seat. I watched them interact with a soft smile. Bowen's gruff exterior hadn't stood a chance against Annie's charming personality, and it was more clear to me than ever before just how much of himself he'd locked away after the incident. The stories about him before hadn't done him justice, and the stories after, were laughable in the face of the man I'd come to know.

When the carriage finally stopped in front of the manor, Annie leaped from the vehicle and scurried up the steps. Her mad dash ground to a halt when the front door opened and a man stared down at her. She peered back up at him.

"Are you the butler, sir? I've never had a butler before."

Gavin flattened his lips and glared at Bowen. "Did you tell this little goblin I was a butler?" He turned his attention back to Annie. "I'm not your butler. I'm just staying here till I get back on my feet."

"You're already on your feet, sir."

"Already on my feet?" Gavin scoffed. "Who are you anyway?"

"Annie Bauer. Who are you?"

"Gavin."

She tested the name on her lips, decided she liked it, and then gave a nod of approval. "You're not as tall as Bowen, and you don't have any distinguishing marks, but I won't hold it against you."

"You won't hold it against me?" He gave her an incredulous look.

Bowen climbed the steps and clapped Gavin on the back. "She lives here now. Be nice, or I'll give her your room." He walked past him into the house, ignoring Gavin's look of surprise.

Gavin's mouth worked like a fish, all air and no words. "I've died. I actually drank too much, and now I'm dead. Can you see me?" He addressed Annie again, who giggled and rushed past him to chase after Bowen.

"You're not a ghost, Gavin," I said, putting him out of his misery.

He shook his head, scrubbing a hand over his face. "There goes the rest of my mornings. Children are notoriously early risers. Like someone else I know."

I patted him on the shoulder. "Drink less, Gavin. It will help with that."

His face grew serious, and he fixed me with a penetrating stare. He snagged my arm when I went to move past him, his fingers encircling my wrist. His voice dropped low, tone sharp as he held my gaze.

"You don't know anything about me. But I've been watching you since you arrived. You're changing him, and it seems to be for the better. But what happens when you leave? Don't be cruel. He's been through enough."

Gavin let go of my arm and vanished into the house, leaving me standing in the doorway, reeling from his harsh words of warning. I'd be lying if I hadn't asked myself the same questions. *What happens when I leave?* From somewhere deeper in the house, I heard Annie's screech of excitement, followed by Bowen's rumble of laughter, and I exhaled a shuddering breath.

We were in uncharted territory, getting deeper and deeper to the point of no return. If it wasn't already too late. For the first time, I wondered how it would all end.

A shiver of foreboding climbed my spine.

Because nothing good ever came from an ending.

Chapter 18

Bowen

A layer of frost spiderwebbed the window overlooking the grounds, and I bent to peer through the glass. The scene below was fractured by vines of ice, but even the thick panes and frozen crystals did little to conceal the laughter floating in the air.

Annie ran through the snow, a red scarf flying in the wind behind her. She jerked to a stop, reared back, and threw a snowball at Jacob with all her might. Jacob ducked, but the frosty cannonball clipped him in the shoulder. He grabbed the hit appendage and made an exaggerated tumble into the snow.

More laughter filled the air, this time as both Annie and Liana collapsed into the snow next to Jacob. Their arms and legs moved in wide arcs, and when they climbed to their feet, they'd left behind three snow angel impressions.

"I hope you know what you're doing." Gavin's uneasy voice sounded behind me. He approached, but I didn't take my gaze away from the window.

"And what is it you think I'm doing?"

He leaned against the wall, staring out an adjacent window. "It doesn't take much to look at you and know you want to keep them."

I sighed, and the warmth of my breath fogged the glass, obscuring the scene below. "They're not a pair of rare broadswords to add to my collection, Gavin."

"No, they're not. They can't be bought, cheated, or stolen. Yet that's exactly what you've done. Liana doesn't know the truth about how she came to be here, and they'll probably name a wing after you at the orphanage considering the enormous donation you made to secure Annie's freedom."

"You would rather I left that child to fend for herself and likely encounter the same fate as her brother?"

"Of course not."

"Then what's your point?"

Gavin crossed his arms over his chest. "The house you're building is unstable. I can't believe I'm saying this, but you should tell Liana the truth about what we did to her father to bring her here."

"She won't understand."

"Won't she? The things we do, the darkest parts of us...doesn't she understand that better than anyone?"

"Exactly!" My fist hit the wall near the window, rattling the panes. "She'll understand I manipulated her father, had him locked up, and branded him a thief. I took his freedom away as well as hers. It was the worst thing I could have done considering her past."

"So it's back to the original plan? Send Liana—

and now Annie—back home when the time comes. Destroy the Grimm's blade and ruin Argus, potentially starting a war between you two. What does that leave you with? Have you ever thought about what comes after your revenge?"

"It never mattered before."

"Well, it matters now." Gavin clapped a hand over my shoulder. "I've supported your plan from the beginning, even participated wholeheartedly, but maybe we're wrong. Maybe there's another way. Think about it."

I shook off Gavin's hand and rounded my desk, pulling a jacket from the coat stand. "I'll tell Liana the truth when I think she's ready to hear it." Shrugging into my coat, I crossed the room and stepped into the hall. Gavin's voice echoed behind me.

"It will be too late then, Bowen. You know as well as I do. You're making a mistake."

***

I followed the laughter.

Breathing in the biting cold air, I walked around the side of the manor, boots crunching through the snow. Flurries drifted in the air, light now, but the cloud bank on the horizon promised more to come.

Gavin's words echoed in my mind. He had a point, but it wasn't that simple. If I gave up my plan to hurt Argus and told Liana the truth and she still went home, then I'd be left with nothing. After everything I'd been through, I wasn't sure if I could gamble with those odds.

Of course I wanted them to stay. But at what cost? I'd already lost everything once, and now I was supposed to risk it all again. It was a lot to ask of someone who'd been burned the way I had.

The anger and uncertainty that had me conflicted faded as I caught sight of Liana playing with the others in the snow. She turned as I approached, her eyes lighting up.

"We were wondering if you planned to join us." Her breath came out in white puffs, crystallizing as she spoke. Flurries clung to her eyelashes and caught in the wisps of her hair. I reached out and tucked a blonde curl back behind her ear.

"Well, I can't let you have all the fun."

She scoffed. "Says the recluse."

I wrapped an arm around her shoulder and leaned close to whisper, "I thought we cleared that whole recluse thing up already."

Annie waved a hand through the air, trying to get our attention. She wobbled through the snow until she reached us. "Ask him, Liana! Ask him."

Liana sighed and gazed up at me. "She wants to know if we can go down to the water's edge. I wasn't sure if there was a less slippery path."

I crouched down to Annie's level. "You want to see the water?"

"Yes, please! I've never seen the ocean up close, but my brother says you can find shells in the sand. Is that true?"

"It is. We'll have to see if we can find some. The path down to the water is around the backside of the house. Let's all go."

Annie pressed her mittened hands together in excitement. She shouted over her shoulder. "Did you hear that, Jacob? We're going down to the water! I bet I can find way more seashells than you can. Race you down there!"

She sprinted through the snow, forcing Jacob to chase after her. When he caught up, he grabbed her hand and scolded her about running across the icy path. Together, they made their way toward the water.

I held out my hand. "Shall we?"

Liana intertwined her fingers with mine, and we walked down the man-made path that led to the rocky beach. Annie was already searching between the stones, dodging the ocean spray, searching for shells. Jacob hovered over her, making sure she didn't trip and fall into the water. He'd taken to her right away, assuming the role of a protective older brother. It hadn't been that long, but where one went, the other followed.

"Do you think Annie knows about her ability with magic?" I asked, watching the waves as they crashed ashore.

"No, probably not. It's a strange gift. I didn't have a clue until I came into contact with magic for the first time, and unless you have someone who recognizes the mark and can show you how it works, there's no way to know."

"Annie's lucky then. She'll have you."

Liana sighed. "I just wish I knew why this is happening again. Obviously, the witch wants to use our ability in some way, but for what?"

"That's part of the puzzle we have to figure out. Ethan might have mentioned something to Annie that we don't know about yet, but I think our best chance lies in speaking with someone familiar with a broader world of magic."

"Are you suggesting we meet with another witch? Don't tell me you know one as one of your mysterious connections."

I chuckled. "No, I don't know any other witches. But I'm sure we can find one. It's a big kingdom." My tone grew serious. "Do you think that's something you would be willing to try?"

Liana shivered and rubbed her hands together. The wind whipped her hair around her face, and I reached out to adjust the collar on her jacket to keep the air off her neck. "If it means putting an end to this nightmare, I'll do whatever I have to. I know not all witches are bad." She gave me a weak smile. "Just don't ask me to eat any of their cooking, and if they offer dessert, run."

"Sound advice."

"Liana! Come look!" Annie bent over the sand, unearthing something with a stick.

"I think she found her first shell." Liana smiled, then she narrowed her eyes with sneaky suspicion. "Unless, of course, there's buried treasure out there. You didn't happen to stash a chest of gold coins in the sand, did you? Because I'm a huge proponent of finders keepers."

I shook my head and suppressed a grin. "No. I keep

my fortune stuffed under the mattress like a normal person."

She threw back her head and laughed. "Good to know."

Liana left me standing at the bottom of the path and went to investigate Annie's discovery. They dodged the waves, squealing in delight as the cold water rushed into the hole Annie had created. I watched as they rinsed off their find and started searching the ground for more shells.

It was getting colder, and we'd have to go back inside soon, but I was reluctant to call them back, contented to watch them enjoy the beach. Behind me, boots crunched over the rocky path, and I knew instinctively our pleasant interlude was coming to an end. Gavin stopped beside me, huddled beneath his jacket. He handed me a folded message.

"What happened?" I asked.

"The message is from one of the men you sent to watch the orphanage. Ethan showed up at Ever Haven this morning looking for his sister. When he learned she was gone, he became enraged. They tried to contain him, but he ran. Your men chased him as far as the forest, but then they lost his trail."

I clenched the note in my hand, crinkling the paper. We both stood for a moment in silence, watching the threesome scour the sand for treasure left by the sea.

"What's our next move, Bowen?"

"Tomorrow, we move our search to the woods."

Chapter 19

Bowen

"So, to recap, we got nowhere today." Gavin slumped into a chair and stretched, crossing his booted feet at the ankles.

Leaning heavily against my desk, I tried to rub away the headache pounding my temples. Earlier, we'd visited the orphanage to get an in-person account of what happened when Ethan appeared looking for his sister. But in the end, we learned nothing new. He was in the wind, either having gone back to the witch or maybe still on the hunt for Annie.

We spent the next hours searching the forest where my men had lost track of Ethan. A fresh layer of snow hampered our efforts, and when evening fell, we had to give up our search.

"Maybe we should send the girl away until this blows over. It'll give us more time to keep searching," Gavin said, bringing up the topic we'd been hedging around since yesterday.

I hated the idea even if it made sense. I'd like to think Annie was safest with us watching over her. But maybe she wasn't. Maybe removing her from the kingdom was the best option.

I sighed. "I'll think about it. If it becomes necessary, I'll make arrangements."

"I'd hate to see the little scamp go, but at least I'd be able to catch up on my sleep." His grin seemed forced. Gavin wouldn't outright admit it, but he'd been instantly charmed by Annie. We all had, and we'd do whatever it took to keep her out of harm's way. Groaning, he pushed to his feet. "Speaking of sleep, it's late. I'm calling it. We can search again tomorrow if you want. Maybe we'll get lucky."

Silence settled in as Gavin left the room. I dropped into the chair he'd vacated and let my eyes drift closed. It was late, and I should turn in too, but I was restless. So much seemed out of my control, and I'd spent the past few years doing everything I could to maintain control. To keep from falling deeper into that black abyss. Now, all the old wounds were open, and they were healing, but it was painful and terrifying.

In an impossible turn of events, Gavin had become the fountain of wisdom, and guilt ate at me for not telling Liana the truth about her father. It all felt a little too precarious. One misstep, and the building blocks would fall. What if she took Annie and left? Without the two of them, where would that leave me? It was selfish as hell, but I never claimed to be a saint. I just kept thinking if everything worked out, if we found her brother, kept Annie safe, and stopped the witch, my deception would seem tiny in comparison. She might laugh it off as one of my roughish misdeeds.

It was pure insanity, and I knew it.

A muffled sound near the door pulled me out of my thoughts. I opened my eyes.

"Um…excuse me." Annie stood in the doorway, a threadbare blanket clutched between her fingers. The ends trailed along the floor as she took a cautious step into the room.

"Annie, what are you doing awake? You shouldn't be wandering around on your own."

"I had a bad dream." She sniffled, and I realized she'd been crying. I wasn't sure what to do. The little girl looked so sad. I opened my mouth to respond but hesitated, feeling wholly out of my element.

"I'll go wake Liana."

Annie shook her head, brown pigtails swinging around her cheeks. She walked farther into the room, still dragging the blanket behind her.

It was an odd sort of thing, watching an innocent child cross the threshold to my office. Curiosity and trust were evident in her exploration, and my first thought was thankfully she wasn't tall enough to reach anything hanging on the walls. The scene seemed to unfold as if I were watching it from above. During my treasure hunting days, having a family was a far-off event that would only hinder my fearless lifestyle. After my last expedition, the idea died altogether. Who could have imagined I'd have one temporarily bestowed upon me?

She stopped in front of me and dug her toes into the floor, looking timid. "Can you tell me a story?"

"A story?" I swallowed against the panic creeping up my throat. Did I even know any stories appropriate for children? "Um, sure."

Annie beamed and swiped at the lingering tears under her eyes. I gestured to the chair next to mine, but instead, she shot forward and climbed into my lap. I froze as she situated herself into a comfortable position and tucked the blanket between her head and my chest like a pillow.

Almost a full minute of silence passed before she cleared her throat. "Go ahead. I'm ready."

"Right, of course." I stumbled over the words, racking my brain for a suitable story that didn't end in a prison riot or stranding your competition on a desert island. If Liana were here, she'd know what to say. She probably had a million age-appropriate stories full of wonder that would entertain a child. Besides my dubious adventures, what did I have except for detailed instructions on the uses of battle axes throughout history?

I guessed I'd have to make things up as I went.

"Well..." I cleared the hoarseness from my throat.

"Wait!" Annie looked up, nearly dislodging my chin with the top of her head. "Will this story have dragons?"

Dragons? She's lucky if the story has a beginning, middle, and end.

"No."

She frowned, flattening her lips in displeasure. "Could you add a dragon then?"

Add a dragon? I heaved a sigh. "Fine. Where was I?"

"What about a prince? Does the story have a prince?" She blinked, waiting for my answer.

"You want a prince and a dragon now?"

She flashed her teeth. "And a princess. You can't have a prince without a princess."

"That would be blasphemous," I grumbled, repositioning her so my arm wouldn't fall asleep. The damn thing was already halfway to being numb. "Okay, here we go. Are you ready?"

She gave a curt nod.

"Once upon—"

"I like giants too. And ogres. Elves, but only if they're friendly."

"Do you want to tell the story? Stop interrupting!"

Her gaze narrowed, and she thumped the blanket, snuggling deeper. "I was letting you tell it."

I squeezed my eyes shut at the absurdity of our situation. At this rate, the sun would rise before we'd finished listing characters. Were all children this challenging, or was I just that lucky?

"As I was saying…" I paused, preparing myself for another disruption. When it didn't come, I breathed in relief and continued. "Once upon a time, there was a prince, princess, a dragon, two giants, four ogres, and a band of friendly elves."

A gentle snore rumbled against my chest. I looked down in disbelief. Annie was fast asleep, her thumb stuck between her teeth.

"You're kidding me," I whispered, carefully removing her thumb and tucking it against her side. "I didn't even get to the good part."

"You can tell it to me."

My attention snapped to the entrance where Liana

lounged against the wall. Her arms were crossed over her shoulders, and a beautiful smile played at her lips.

"That depends on whether you have a list of demands too. How long have you been standing there?"

"Long enough to know you had no story planned beyond the first line."

"Was it that obvious?"

She stepped away from the wall, moving closer. Her bare feet were soft on the carpet. The firelight played over her features, making her hair shimmer, and there was a look in her eyes—something I'd never seen before but definitely wanted to see again.

"I'm sure you would have come up with something." She knelt beside the chair and smoothed a lock of hair from Annie's face. "Did you get any more information from the orphanage?"

"No. It was a dead end. When Ethan found out his sister was no longer there, he got spooked. One of the attendants chased after him, but they lost him in the streets. Gavin and I spent some time searching on foot, but we didn't get any leads."

She stifled a yawn. "Then I guess we keep at it until we find them. Eventually, someone will have seen something."

"You look tired. You should get some rest." My gaze dropped to Annie. "Save yourself. I've lost all feeling in my arm."

She chuckled, and a mischievous glint flashed in her eyes. "But I want to know more about your story. You mentioned it has a prince, and a princess, giants, ogres, and elves. That's quite the cast of characters."

"You forgot dragons," I murmured.

"That's right. How could I forget? But what about the ending? Do they all live happily ever after?"

"Is that your story demand?"

She shook her head, and the smile slipped from her lips. Moving toward the hearth, she splayed her fingers over the flames, soaking up the warmth. "I always skip the end of the story. Who really lives happily ever after? It's something we tell children to shield them from the horrors of the world."

I painstakingly shifted Annie to the chair, doing my best not to wake her. I shouldn't have worried. It seemed my brief attempt at a bedtime story had knocked her out cold. I joined Liana by the hearth. She let me wrap my arms around her, and she rested her head against my shoulder, staring at the flames.

"Do you really believe that?" I asked.

She exhaled long and slow. "I don't know anymore. I've started to think maybe it's the horrors that earn us our happily ever after. Maybe it's the only way to tell if we deserve one or not."

The snap and crack of the flames filled in the void created by our silence. I wasn't sure how to respond or if she even wanted me to. A long moment passed before she gestured toward Annie.

"Do you want me to take her?"

"No. I'll take her back to her room. Who knows? She might wake up and demand a story about mermaids. I'll have to be ready."

Liana furrowed her brow. "Do you know any

stories about mermaids?"

"Not one." I dropped a kiss on her forehead and went to retrieve Annie. I picked her up and slung her blanket over my shoulder. Lowering my voice so as not to wake her, I said, "Tomorrow, Gavin and I will pick up the search where we left off. We're going to find them. I promise."

"I don't know how to thank you for everything you've done. I know things started rocky with my father, and I—"

"Don't thank me, Liana." A fresh wave of guilt pricked my conscience.

She nodded and whispered goodnight. With her misplaced praise ringing in my ears, I escaped into the hallway.

Soon. I'll tell her the truth soon. Just not tonight.

Chapter 20

Liana

I tiptoed down the dark hallway toward my room, thankful, for the first time in my life, for the shadows that masked the silly grin on my face. Watching Bowen attempt to tell Annie a bedtime story was not the scene I expected to walk into when I went to check on how the search had gone and say goodnight, but it was one I was glad I didn't miss.

It was strange to think about stories again. After all these years, I never expected I might get an ending to the events from my past. It always seemed as if it would remain this open-ended thing that happened to me with no real closure. Even though I'd moved on the best I could, that lack of closure, the not knowing, made it difficult to find peace.

We were all looking for closure in our own ways. Bowen was still struggling to find himself after the pain inflicted upon him, and even—

I blinked, squinting down the shadowed hallway. Was that Gavin?

At the far end of the hall, I spotted a figure turning the corner. The faint glow of a lantern illuminated

Gavin's grim features as he headed toward the east wing. There wasn't anything of interest in that direction besides the glass-enclosed training room, and I wondered why he would go up there so late at night.

Pausing outside my room, I remembered his blunt words from the other day. It felt as if the message had come out of nowhere, but maybe it hadn't. He was obviously a loyal friend to Bowen and was concerned about our growing relationship. I wasn't sure I could blame him. The last thing I expected was to develop feelings for Bowen MacKenzie, and the same question of what would happen when it was time for me to go home had plagued my thoughts. Still, if he thought I was using Bowen, seducing him for my own purpose, I wasn't sure I was okay with that.

Bypassing my room, I followed him up to the domed training area.

Moonlight shimmered through the glass panes, washing the room in silver. Gavin stood facing the sea, completely motionless. His gaze seemed fixed on the horizon. In his hand was a glass bottle filled halfway with a ruby liquid. An odd choice since he always favored whiskey or rum.

He popped the cork and took a swig, then he held the bottle at an angle, almost as if he were toasting the horizon. I moved closer, my feet silent on the polished floor, and watched as he removed a small object from his pocket. He held it in his open palm, and at first, I thought it was a stone, but upon closer inspection, I realized it was smoother and slightly translucent. A victim of the waves, tossed until the edges had been refined and the surface given a frosted sheen.

Sea glass.

I'd only come across glass like that a few times before, and it had always surprised me to see the way nature exerted its force, turning something sharp and jagged into an almost velvety work of art. I supposed time and the right conditions had a way of doing that.

Still oblivious to my presence, Gavin rubbed the sea glass between his fingers, then he closed it in his fist. His head dropped to his chest, and the bottle hung limply from his hand.

"Gavin," I murmured, afraid I'd startle him.

He whirled, and his gaze raked over me. Confusion laced his scrutiny, and for a moment, he looked dazed. His skin paled, and he inhaled a sharp breath.

"Marin?" The name was soft on his lips, almost a plea instead of a question.

"No, it's Liana. I didn't mean to disturb you."

Recognition flooded his features, and he stuffed the sea glass back into his pocket. "What are you doing up here? It's late."

The resignation in his tone almost compelled me to ask who the mysterious Marin was and if she was the reason he preferred to spend his nights curled up next to a bottle. But something in his eyes told me not to go there.

Instead, I feigned ignorance. "I couldn't sleep. I thought coming up here and watching the waves might relax me." I gestured toward the wine bottle. "But maybe I should try your remedy."

His harsh laugh scraped through the air. "It's no remedy, but it gets the job done." He offered me the bottle, daring me to take it.

I did and took a deep swig of the fruity wine.

"You're full of surprises, Liana. You don't seem the type to drown your sorrows."

I took another pull from the bottle and handed it back. "Well, like you said the other day, you don't know anything about me."

He swirled the wine in the bottle, a smirk curling his mouth. "I know enough. I know things are different around here because of you. I know Bowen's thirst for revenge against Argus is waning and his priorities are shifting. I know it's the best thing for him, and yet the greatest risk. Greater than sparking a feud with a criminal organization. Greater than letting him while away his days hunkered down in the manor."

"And why is that?"

"Because it's obvious he's falling for you—or fallen, as the case may be." He nodded and took a swig from the bottle. "Definitely past tense. This wasn't part of the plan, but there it is. Love, the great healer of wounds." The cynical smile slipped from his lips. "Ironically, also the great inflictor of pain."

He spoke as if from experience, passing the bottle back to me. My fingers wrapped tightly around the base while I absorbed his words. The fluttery feeling inside my belly had nothing to do with the wine and everything to do with hoping Gavin was right. But I couldn't deny the truth in his statement. After I failed to save Hendrik, I thought I didn't deserve forgiveness or love, and yet Sarah and Thomas gave it to me anyway. I was sure if they hadn't, I would have ended up exactly like Bowen.

When I let the silence continue to drag, Gavin started to pace the floor and filled it.

"You know, I helped him plan his revenge against Argus. The whole thing. We laughed about seeing his face when Bowen destroyed the Grimm's blade. Neither of us cared or even thought about the consequences."

"But you're thinking about them now?"

Gavin tapped his foot nervously against the floor and scrubbed a hand through his disheveled hair. "Argus needs the blade to help his sister, and he's using the newly minted oracle Vivian James to track the blade. Bowen knows, and I think he wishes there was a way he could just let it all go. Somehow, things got complicated, and it's not just Argus on the line anymore. Bowen's not a bad man—you know that—but sometimes, it's nearly impossible to make the right choice."

"I see. So how do we help him?"

"I'm not sure. It feels as if things are spinning out of control, and I—"

Footsteps pounded through the chamber leading to the training room. A man appeared holding a wooden club in his hands. He approached Gavin.

"What is it, Deacon?"

"I've been looking for you. Two people were spotted earlier on the property, near the cliffs. A man and a woman. It looks as if they entered the manor from one of the old shipping tunnels."

Gavin cursed and closed his eyes as if trying to think. "It has to be Argus and the oracle. This is some miserable timing. Have you told Bowen?"

"Yes. He secured the little girl with Ms. Wilder and then went looking for them. He tracked the man to his office, but the woman was nowhere to be found."

"Which means she's still somewhere inside the manor. She'll probably end up skewered on a piece of his collection."

I took a final fortifying sip of wine and tossed Gavin what was left in the bottle. "I'll go and find her. It can't be too late. There must be something we can do to stop this."

Gavin nodded. "If Bowen has Argus, he'll have taken him down to the forge where he'll destroy the Grimm's blade. You need to get to Vivian first and get her out of here. I'll handle Bowen."

***

I watched the woman from the shadows. She'd found her way down to the gallery, somehow meeting Brutus along the way. The dog padded after her, nudging the back of her thigh, clearly in search of treats or attention. A knot of nerves tightened in my stomach as she approached the glass case holding the mystical dagger.

So much was at stake—for all involved. I wanted Bowen free of his drive for revenge and the ability for his past to harm any part of his future. But also, if

Argus needed the Grimm's blade to save his sister, I couldn't help but feel a certain level of understanding. There were no true villains here, only people caught inside forces beyond their control.

There wasn't much time. I had to get Vivian out of here before someone else came to retrieve the blade.

"So much for the guard dog. Brutus, come here." I held out my hand as Brutus whirled and trotted toward me. He sank beside me and licked my palm.

Vivian looked startled, not only by being discovered but at the loss of her furry companion. "Who are you?" she asked.

It was a strange question for an intruder to ask, and it made me laugh. "Don't you think I should be asking you that, considering you're in my home?"

Her stunned expression turned into wide-eyed horror. "You live here? With Bowen the Beast?"

I *really* hated that nickname.

"I do. For the time being. I'm Liana Archer. My father ran into a bit of legal trouble with Bowen, and I ended up taking his place. Of course, that explains why I'm here, but not why you're here, Vivian."

"I didn't give you my name." Wariness lurked in her tone, and she took a cautious step back.

"No, you didn't. But you didn't have to. I've known for a while you'd come for the Grimm's blade. It was all part of his plan. Though, trap might be a more appropriate term. He really doesn't like your friend."

"Trap? You mean, Bowen planned this?" Her features tightened, and her gaze darted back the way she'd come.

"Relax. I don't approve of what he's done." I walked past her and lifted the glass surrounding the Grimm's blade. The familiar dagger's gemstones winked in the candlelight. "Take it. You'll need a direct hit to the heart—nothing else will do."

"How do you know that?"

My lips thinned as I recalled the original reason I crafted the blade. A few years ago, I was hired to help save a village overrun with vicious beasts. They'd needed a Grimm's blade made of enchanted steel and had sought out my services. The village was successful in defeating the beasts, and since the magic source used to create the dagger was so rare, whenever there was a need for the blade, Thomas acted as the intermediary to broker the transfer of the weapon. Who could have ever imagined it would end up here, a pawn in a long-standing feud?

"I have some experience with weapons like this. The monsters you seek are drawn to the blade. They'll stop at nothing to reclaim it and secure their bloodline."

"I don't understand. Why are you helping me? What if Bowen finds out?"

I drew in a deep breath, fully aware of the risk I was taking. The risk of the consequences to this moment, and the risk to my heart.

"I have my reasons."

Vivian shook her head and waved her arm through the air. "If Bowen is keeping you here, let us help you. Come with us."

A soft smile formed on my lips. "I can't leave. I

made a promise, and I won't go back on my word. But he's not all bad. He's been kind." *Kinder than I ever imagined he could be.* "Sometimes, I look at him and catch glimpses of the man he used to be, and I have hope."

Vivian reached out and clasped my hand. A strange emotion filtered across her features, and I almost think she understood the feeling. We were both quiet for a moment until footsteps came thundering down the stairs. Brutus whined and nudged his nose into my skirt.

We were too late!

"Quick! Someone's coming." I tugged on her arm, but she reached inside a satchel hanging from her shoulder. My lips parted as she withdrew a blade almost identical to the one sitting on the pedestal. She quickly swapped them out, then she hurried with me into the shadows behind a cabinet of wooden spears.

I recognized Gavin as he slowed near the glass case. His gaze darted around the room. I shifted slightly out of the shadows, and his eyes found mine. When I gave him a subtle nod, he wasted no time collecting the decoy before turning on his heel and heading back up the stairs.

"That was close," I whispered. "You'd better hurry. If he sent someone to get the blade, it means he's found your friend. He'll be keeping him in his workshop. I'll show you the way and distract Bowen so you two have enough time to get out."

"Thank you, Liana. I don't know what to say except I hope one day, we'll be able to meet again. Under more pleasant circumstances."

A hysterical laugh bubbled in my throat. "You mean, when we're not in a cavern full of weapons while the master of the house holds your friend hostage?"

She grinned. "Exactly."

We followed the darkened corridors leading toward the forge. Before we parted ways, Vivian placed her hand on my arm.

"I owe you, and if you ever need anything, I'll repay the favor. For the time being, you can get word to me through the magic shop."

"The magic shop?"

"Yeah. Tessa Daniels, the kingdom's witch, owns the place. She'll know how to find me. Anything either one of us can do, just let us know." She smiled and squeezed my arm. "Take care, Liana."

I nodded and watched as she slipped away into the shadows. A buzz flowed through my veins. Vivian knew a witch?

We needed information, and Tessa Daniels might be exactly the witch to give it.

But first, I needed to find Bowen.

Chapter 21

Bowen

The heat from the forge radiated against my back as I waited for the unconscious man chained to the wall to awaken. I ran the edge of a sword over a whetstone, letting the slice of metal against rock drown out the noise inside my head.

I'd waited for this moment for years—had set the plan into motion myself—yet so far, I'd found little satisfaction in the act. This was supposed to be the moment I took back control of my life and made Argus pay for his part in my downfall. It was supposed to feel exhilarating and cleansing. I never imagined I'd feel shame. But there it was, clawing to get out.

Did I really think I could punish Argus with the same savageness I had been shown? I once told Liana I craved the power my weapons collection afforded me, and she didn't seem surprised. She was someone who never wanted to be at a disadvantage and had honed her skills with the intent to never let it happen. But after meeting her, it didn't take long for me to realize I'd rather spend my time protecting her than waste it mired in the past.

Argus jerked awake and winced at the pain likely pounding through his skull. I'd cornered him in my office, finding him alone, even though I knew he'd arrived with the oracle. Somehow, they'd gotten separated. Regardless of her involvement, my payback didn't include her.

"That's gonna leave a mark." I paused in the act of sharpening the blade to angle it at the side of Argus's head where one of my men had knocked him out cold. "It'll fade though, unlike these." My fingers stroked the jagged scars along my cheekbone.

"How long was I out?" he asked.

"Does it matter?" I chuckled, knowing he was probably wondering what had happened to the oracle.

"How long?" he growled, yanking on the chains binding his wrists to the wall.

"You're not asking the right questions. It's disappointing." I dropped the sword onto a table and turned my attention to the man who'd helped me drag Argus to the forge. I'd sent someone to find Gavin, but he hadn't shown yet. There was no sense in waiting any longer. I wanted this done. "Bring me the Grimm's blade."

"Yes, sir." The heavily reinforced door creaked open as the man slipped through, leaving me alone with Argus.

I grabbed the sword and approached a crucible hanging over the heated forge. Thrusting the blade into the red-hot coals, I watched as the metal heated.

"You and I go way back, don't we? We have a history of getting in each other's way."

"Hazards of the trade," Argus said, trying to shift into a more comfortable position.

I smirked. "No doubt. But there's one encounter I want to make sure you remember. Because it's one I've never been able to forget."

"I don't know what you're talking about."

And that was part of the problem. It was so easy to hate someone oblivious to your pain and their part in afflicting it.

"Of course you don't. Why would you? You were always so obsessed with ruining your father's empire you never stopped to think about who else could get caught up in your plans. You know, it wasn't long ago that I was just like you—always looking for the next score, walking over anyone in my way as long as I got to the treasure first. As you can see, it didn't work out for me."

"Enough of your vague ramblings. If you knew I was searching for the blade, why did you buy it out from under me? Why go through all the trouble?"

I hooked my fingers in my leather belt and leaned against the worktable. "Because you ruined my life by setting fire to the one object I spent years searching for, and this seemed like the perfect opportunity to return the favor."

Argus's brow creased in confusion. "The warehouse fire?"

"Very good. You do remember. I'd just returned from overseas, and the shipment I brought back had been offloaded into your father's warehouse. He hired me to find the Incantus."

"The fabled treasure chest? What did my father want with it?"

"It wasn't for him. It was for the witch."

"What witch?"

My brow rose. "You don't know? That's a surprise. Robert visited a witch to help him find a cure for his illness. The witch promised him immortality, but she wanted the Incantus as payment. That's where I came in. I found the chest. It was the greatest achievement of my career, and it wasn't even about the money; it was the prestige."

Selecting a short, thin blade off the worktable, I turned it in my hand and paced the stone floor.

"The night of the fire, I went to retrieve it but found the building already engulfed in flames. I nearly died in that fire trying to get to the treasure. The building was a total loss, everything inside either burned or scavenged by the men who tried to put out the flames. The contents of the chest were gone. Robert blamed me for setting the fire. He thought I'd decided to keep the treasure for myself. He tortured me. He gave me these." I swiped a hand down the side of my face, ending at the base of my scars. "It wasn't until much later I discovered it was you who'd burned the warehouse."

Approaching Argus, I crouched down, twisting the knife so the metal gleamed in the torchlight.

"Do you have any idea what it feels like when hot metal slides through your skin? The searing pain that stops your breath? The screams you can't contain? Screams that ring in your nightmares long after it's over... Pain like that does something to your soul. It corrodes it until there's nothing good left."

"I didn't know. You were never the target."

"Maybe not, but it doesn't matter. I couldn't let it go, and when I found out you were desperately searching for the Grimm's blade, I took it, and now, I'm going to destroy it while you watch. I lost my treasure, and you'll lose yours."

"Don't do this," Argus grated.

I stood and gave him my back. More of that shame slid like oil inside my veins. I felt nauseous. If I went through with this and destroyed the blade, I would be ruining any chance Argus had of saving his sister. If Liana were standing next to me right now, I don't think she'd be proud.

But what choice did I have?

To give it all up now without at least making him feel a shred of the suffering I had to live through felt like an injustice. There had to be something. There had to be a way...

The door swung open, and Gavin entered. In his hand, he held the Grimm's blade. There was a look in his eye as he handed it over—something that made me hesitate. He'd been warning me for days about the consequences of this moment, and I sensed that warning again, but this time, something was off.

"Ah, it's here." I accepted the weapon, feeling the weight of it in my hand. The jewels glittered in the firelight, and I ran my thumb slowly over the hilt then along the edge of the blade.

Wait a second...

The dagger looked exactly as it should, but it *felt* different. My gaze found Gavin's, and he returned the stare. Suddenly, I knew. The oracle. She'd switched out the original with a replica. A good replica at that, but not good enough to fool me.

I almost laughed. This was it. This was the moment I'd been waiting for all these years. I walked toward the forge and held the dagger over the crucible. Argus rattled the chains, desperation painted over his features. He had no way of knowing whether the blade I had was the fake, and his misery was real.

Misery for misery. A perfect ending. I'd be set free without consequence and without shame.

Still, might as well have a little fun.

"You know, I planned on dragging this out. All this time, my revenge against you kept me going. It was all I wanted, all I could think about." I paused for effect, watching Argus squirm. "But life has a funny way of changing your priorities."

"What are you saying?"

I smiled. Not a smile meant to induce fear, but one that underscored the truth in my words.

"There's something I want more than this. I didn't think that was possible, but she's waiting for me downstairs."

"Don't touch her."

Ah, he thinks I mean the oracle. How amusing.

The masterpiece of this entire endeavor was that he thought I was about to destroy the blade and take his woman. Liana was right: I was bloodthirsty.

"This ends tonight. It's time for me to let go and

look toward the future." I released the blade, watching as it hit the molten iron, floated for a few seconds, and then sank beneath the surface.

The replica was gone forever.

"Your debt is paid." I turned toward the door.

Argus's shout echoed against the walls. "Don't touch her! I'll kill you if you do."

I kept going, my smile widening as the heavy weight that had held me down for years lifted. "You'll be released in the morning. Don't show your face here again."

Gavin walked with me down the stone corridor that led back toward the upper floors of the manor. He clapped a hand on my back and shook his head.

We paused beneath the light of a flickering torch.

"The blade was a fake, Gavin. A good one…a very good one, but a fake all the same."

Chuckling, Gavin swiped a hand through his hair. "I suspected as much. I don't think Liana would have let me take it otherwise."

"Liana knew?"

"I was with her when we found out Argus and the oracle made it inside the manor. After everything that's happened—how far you've come—neither one of us wanted to see this go any further. I asked her to help and sent her to find the oracle. But if you're going to be angry, be angry with me."

"You essentially scuttled my revenge. I should run you through with a rusty spear." My gaze narrowed. "Or better yet, make you get a real job."

"I'll take the spear."

"I thought as much. Lucky for you, I'm not angry. I got what I wanted. What happened to me was meant to bring me to ruin. It was vindictive and cruel. All these years, I let it consume me. But I'm the one who gave it power. Thankfully, a fire goes out if you take away its oxygen." I blew out a breath and raised my gaze to the ceiling. "Listen to me spouting platitudes. Argus didn't know the blade was fake. His misery was real. I enjoyed that part immensely."

Gavin scoffed. "He seemed really put out when you mentioned *her*."

"You noticed that, didn't you? That was fun for me too."

"So what happens now?"

"The hard part. I'm done letting my past rule my life, but there's still the matter of Liana and her father. No more secrets."

"You're right. It's time. Just don't tell her when she's around any weapons. Maybe make her take off her dagger belt. She's not going to be happy to learn you framed her father for theft and had him detained in prison just so you could exploit her into creating that crossbow."

A soft footfall made me tense, and I looked over my shoulder down the dark corridor. Squinting, I tried to make out any movement, but there was nothing there.

"Did you hear that?"

"Hear what?"

"That sound. Like someone moved."

Gavin sighed. "You're hearing things. Liana's busy

wrapping things up with the oracle, Annie is with Ms. Wilder, and Argus is literally chained to the wall. I think we're alone."

Unease made my nerves tingle, but I chalked it up to my upcoming confession. "I'm going to find Liana. Let Argus stew a little longer, and then release him. Make sure both he and the oracle get off my property. Tomorrow's a new day, and I don't want anything from my past to ruin it."

Chapter 22

Liana

I slipped into the shadows.
My fingers dragged across the cold stone wall, using the coarse rock to ground me and lead me away from the voices that echoed in my head.

She's not going to be happy to learn you framed her father for theft and had him detained in prison just so you could exploit her into creating that crossbow.

Acid climbed my throat. How could he? But more to the point, how could I not have known, walking around the manor like a fool for weeks? Was the action worse, or the secret? My stomach churned. Years ago, I was fooled by the witch, lulled by her soothing words and promises of a better life, yet it was a deception. She'd only wanted to use me for my gift. Her deception had cost me everything, and now, here I was again, caught in another web of lies.

I climbed the spiral staircase that led to the domed training room, needing to think. Needing to calm down before I did something I'd regret. I spoke the truth to Vivian earlier: Bowen wasn't all bad. Far from it! And his actions over the past few weeks had made me realize how deeply I cared for him. But he had still manipulated me, taken advantage of my weakness, and robbed me of my freedom for his own purposes.

It wasn't so easily forgiven.

The moonlight shimmered over the surface of the water, and a wave of homesickness rammed me so hard in the gut I nearly doubled over. This wasn't fair! How was I supposed to trust people when they kept exploiting me? When they took whatever they wanted without a care for the people they hurt?

Footsteps sounded behind me, and I tensed as I heard Bowen's voice.

"Liana? We need to talk."

A knot of anguish unspooled in my stomach. I had to know the truth, hear it from his lips. Was he the man I'd fallen in love with, or the enemy?

I didn't face him. Instead, I moved toward the rack holding the sabers we'd fought with when I first came to the manor. I selected one and slid another across the floor. It skittered to a stop under his boot.

"What are you doing?" he asked, staring down at the weapon. "Did something happen?" Concern laced his tone, and I tried to harden myself against it.

Fool me once, shame on you. Fool me twice, shame on me. Three times, and I'll run you through.

I examined the saber, twisting the hilt with my wrist. "Revenge is such a funny thing."

"I don't understand what you mean."

"I heard you downstairs. You lied to me about my father and about how I came to be here, and I'm starting to think maybe you lied about everything else too."

His voice dipped, and he took a step forward, reaching out his hand. "No, that's not true."

"Did you or did you not frame my father and send him to prison?"

"I did."

My palm felt slick around the hilt of the saber. I tightened my grip as a single tear slid down my cheek. I swiped it away with a violent flick of my hand. Jaw tightening, I lifted the blade and moved into a fighting stance.

"Don't do this, Liana. Let me explain."

"So you can lie to me again? Pick up your weapon."

He bent at the waist, reaching for the blade at his feet. It hung loosely in his grip even as I threatened him with my own weapon. The night wind rattled the windows, and an icy chill raised the gooseflesh on my arms. I felt cold from the inside out, hollow, unsure. The only thing steady was my hand, the saber an extension of my desire to force the truth from him.

Time seemed to stall, then it sped forward double-time as I lunged with the razor's edge of the blade aimed at Bowen's heart. His eyes glinted in the moonlight, never leaving mine as my saber sliced through the air.

He didn't move. My control slipped when I feared he wasn't going to fight back. But no—something shifted in the last second, and his features tightened, muscles clenching with the force of his decision.

Our blades clashed, sending vibrations shooting through my palm and up my arm. This was different than our first fight. There was no playful teasing, no amusement. Neither one of us hid behind coy smiles or a lack of understanding of our opponent.

With our sabers crossed, he shoved me back a step and kept coming. My heart thudded painfully in my chest from the savage look in his eyes. His heavy footsteps pounded against the floor, and I faltered, altering my grip to deflect the blow he thrust toward my shoulder.

"Is this what you wanted? You won't listen to what I have to say, so you'll make me defend myself with steel?" The guttural sound of his voice echoed in my ears, sending a sliver of alarm through my body. Had I pushed him too far or not far enough?

His weapon whistled through the air, and I spun, using a display case to block his next strike. It landed with a clang against the reinforced glass. Taking cover in the shadows, I tried to regain control of my breathing. His footfalls were nearly silent against the polished floor, stalking closer, hunting me with practiced precision. The back of my neck tingled with awareness.

"You lied to me. You used me for your own interests."

"I did," he whispered close to my ear.

Startled, I lunged away, lifting my weapon in defense. He stepped back into the moonlight, and the silver rays bathed his grim features. The scars that made others cower in fear paled in comparison to his fierce gaze.

"I saw something I wanted, and I took it. It's true

your father was merely a tool to get you here, and you know what, Liana?"

"What?" I asked around the tightness in my throat.

"I'd do it again." He closed the distance, the blade gleaming in the moonlight. His weight shifted to the balls of his feet as he readied his next assault.

I struck first, and the hint of a smile crested his lips. He dodged the blow, but I made the mistake of getting too close. His empty hand wrapped around my wrist. Fingers pressed against my pulse, he dragged me roughly against him.

His grip gentled. "If that makes me a monster, then I'm a monster. But I wouldn't change anything, and I know you hate to hear that. You want apologies and an assurance I'm not like the demons from your past." Releasing my wrist, he raised his hand, thumb skating across my jaw and tilting it upward. A tear set itself free, rolling down my cheek until it pooled against the crease where his skin met mine.

"What are you then?" I asked.

"Grateful." The rasp of his voice sent a shiver down my back. "So damned grateful you forced me out of the dark pit I wallowed in for years. I swear, when you look at me, I think the only scars you see are the ones on the inside that haven't started healing until now... until you."

"Bowen—"

"Grateful your pain has made you into the bravest woman I've ever known. The only one who would have traded places with her father, who hasn't given up on her brother, and the only one who picks up a sword when she's angry instead of running away. If you can move on and find a purpose despite your past, then so can I. You've shown me how."

Another tear escaped, and this time, Bowen carefully brushed it away. The anger drained from my body. I could keep fighting, push him away with words and the tip of my blade, but it wouldn't do any good.

Humbled by his confession, I felt my chin wobble, and I cleared the tightness from my throat. My blade lowered to the floor. "You know, I don't think I would have killed you."

First came his relief, then the rumble of laughter. "I'm glad to hear it."

"But what you did hurt me. It hurt my family. I shared everything with you, and you kept secrets."

"I am sorry for that, and it's something I wouldn't do again. I was selfish and blind to anything outside of getting my revenge." He rested his hand on my waist, drawing me closer. "Liana, about tonight... I know you helped the oracle, and I know the Grimm's blade was fake."

The weapon in my hand clattered to the floor. I squeezed my numb fingers into a fist, suddenly feeling like a hypocrite. I'd justified my actions tonight by thinking I knew what was best for him, but really, hadn't I stolen his control? Were my actions any less of a deception than his?

I staggered back a step, putting a safe distance between us while I tried to come up with the words to explain myself. Maybe I shouldn't have dropped my blade. My gaze shifted to the saber at his feet and then back to his face. His brow arched, easily reading my thoughts.

"I couldn't let you go through with it."

"Why?" he asked.

"Because Argus needed the Grimm's blade to help his sister, and I made that dagger to stop evil. I couldn't let it be destroyed."

"I see. Very noble. I would expect nothing less." He stepped over my saber, still holding his, and forced me to retreat another step. "Is that the only reason?"

"No." My spine straightened, and I held my ground until he was so close I could feel the heat from his body. "Mostly, I was afraid one day, you'd wake up and hate yourself for what you did. I was terrified your revenge would cause further retaliation." Slowly, I reached out, past the blade between us, and rested my palm against his cheek. "It broke my heart to think you might always define yourself by your lowest moment. Because the loss of your reputation and the pain from your scars were meant to break you, and maybe they did for a little while, but I don't believe that's still the case. When I look at you, I don't see a broken man."

"What do you see?"

"A talented artist who finds so much beauty in the world around him and somehow captures it on paper. A man who takes in a friend when they're at their most self-destructive."

"Gavin showed up and won't leave. It's not what you think."

"It is what I think. Don't lessen it. You opened your

home to an orphan and took on my burden with no questions asked. I'm not going to let you continue hiding behind these walls, thinking your best days are behind you. Because they're not."

"They're not, huh?"

"No. And if you kick me out, I'll just come back. You think Gavin's a pest? He's got nothing on me. I'll throw out all your stuff—"

"You already did that. You're costing me a fortune in new tools."

I choked on a laugh. "Good. Then I'll go back to tearing down every last curtain. I know I missed a few. You'll never have any peace and quiet."

He dropped his weapon, and his fingers slid through my hair. "I haven't had peace and quiet for weeks."

"Get used to it."

I closed my eyes as his mouth found mine. Liquid heat pooled in my veins as he slanted his head to deepen the kiss. He circled his arms around me, pressing me close. If this was my punishment, I'd take it and then some.

He broke away only long enough to take in a breath—air I desperately needed myself—but the momentary loss made me rock forward, searching for him again. A seductive laugh rumbled in his throat, and he framed his hands against my face, kissing my jawline and trailing lower, sliding down the column of my neck.

"We're a mess," I said, tilting my head as his mouth tickled the shell of my ear.

"A total mess," he groaned, walking me backward until I bumped a display case.

"Lying."

"Stealing," he countered.

"Fighting to the death."

He paused, brows furrowing. "You said you weren't going to kill me."

"Basic rules of fighting. Never trust an angry woman with a sword."

"Noted." A wicked smile curved his lips before he pressed a kiss against my beating pulse, sending tiny shivers through my body. I curled my fingers into his shirt, tugging him closer, needing to feel the feverish pull of his mouth again.

He came willingly, molding his body against mine.

I bit back a moan as his tongue swept into my mouth. Spinning me away from the glass case, he lifted me, arms beneath my thighs, and walked toward the training mat. He lowered me to the cushioned surface, our mouths still fused together.

My hands splayed across his muscled back, smoothed over the ridges of his abdomen, and glided past his collarbone to wrap around his neck. Above my head, the stars glittered through the glass panes, and the darkness that had always infected my life wrapped around me. But this time, I felt safe.

Treasured.

Loved.

His fingers ghosted over my rib cage and tangled with the ties on my bodice. He whispered his intentions, and I nodded as the chilly air caressed my exposed skin. The heat of his mouth followed, and I arched my back, lost to sensation.

***

We lay together, wrapped in each other's arms. Bowen smoothed a hand over my hair and pressed a kiss to my temple.

"You're cold," he whispered. "Next time, we need to reevaluate our surroundings. There's a bearskin rug in front of the hearth."

I chuckled and nuzzled his neck. "You're right. You have weapons in every room. We could have easily fought where it was warmer."

Reluctantly, he reached for our clothes, helping me slip back into my dress. Once clothed, I leaned back against his chest, letting him wrap his arm around my middle.

I covered his hands with mine, rubbing my fingers over his rough skin. "After everything that happened tonight with Argus and the Grimm's blade, are you really okay? I know how significant tonight was for you. I don't take what Gavin and I did lightly."

Bowen dropped his chin onto the top of my head and sighed. "I'll only admit this to you, so you can't tell a soul…" He waited until I nodded, then he gave me a little squeeze for good measure. "Swear on your reputation as a mystical weapons dealer?"

"Of course! I'm not a gossiping goose like you or Gavin." I swallowed a laugh. "Tell me."

"When I realized the Grimm's blade was fake, I was relieved. It was like a message permitting me to just let it all go. And I did. I dropped that fake dagger into the crucible as if it were the real thing. It felt cleansing."

"Did Argus know it was fake?"

"Nope! You should have seen his face. Worth all the trouble. I wish I had my sketch pad."

I elbowed him in the ribs. "Bloodthirsty!"

"Always," he whispered against my hair. He blew out a breath. "So now this is behind us, where do we go from here?"

"Honestly?" A soft smile spread across my lips. "I wish we could just stay in this moment, suspended, for a little while. But I know that's not possible with my brother and Ethan still out there."

"We could keep searching. Make another round to the shops, see if anyone recognized them from the posters."

"Yes, we should do that, but first, I have a different idea." I turned in his arms, tilting my head back until I met his gaze. "The other day, you mentioned we should try to meet with another witch to get as much information as we can. Well, I think I know where to find one who will help us."

"You do?"

"Yeah. When I helped the oracle, she gave me a name and told me to visit her if I ever needed anything." I drew in a breath, steeling myself against the nerves. "If you can face Argus, I can face a witch. Let's turn in the favor and go meet Tessa Daniels."

Chapter 23

Liana

The magic shop looked harmless enough.

Nestled down a narrow lane dotted with similar dwellings, the compact two-story cottage gave off a rustic feel. A wooden gate blocked the entrance, and a short cobblestone path led to a wraparound porch. Perched next to the door was a sign reading, "Daniels Curses, Cures, and Crimes."

"What an odd name for a shop," I muttered, angling my head to peer through the frosted window.

"Apparently, she partners with the royal agency on their cases. Gavin checked her out, and she works with that Detective you met when you arrived in the kingdom."

My eyebrows rose. "Oh, right. The handsome one, Detective Chambers."

Bowen snarled, and his tone was layered with distaste. "He's not that handsome. I think he's rather dull if you ask me. A total stickler for rules." He continued to grumble about the detective's seemingly poor traits under his breath while I tried to contain a knowing smile.

I tuned him out and rubbed my hands together, flexing my fingers in nervous trepidation. I'd only ever met one witch, and that didn't go well. Naturally, they weren't all the same. I knew that! But try telling it to the knot of fear inside my chest. What if they looked similar? Stringy gray hair, dark, soulless eyes, a hooked nose, and yellowed teeth. I shuddered.

"Are you sure you're ready for this? I can talk to her alone if you're not comfortable."

"No, I'm fine. I don't think Vivian would have told me to come here if Tessa was the type of witch to take people hostage and use them for nefarious magical purposes." Squaring my shoulders, I reached for the door handle. "Let's do this."

A bell over the door jingled as we entered.

Inside, one half of the shop was filled with shelves of potions, hanging crystals, and bundles of herbs drying from the rafters. A giant bookcase with ancient-looking tomes rested against one wall. The other half was more formal. There was a desk in the corner with stacks of files, and a chair for visitors. A large dressing screen had been placed between the two spaces, giving the desk area a semblance of privacy.

"Hello! Welcome to Daniels Curses, Cures, and Crimes," a young woman singsonged from somewhere in the back of the shop. "I'll be right out. Just waiting for this cauldron to finish bubbling. The last time I left it unattended, there was an incident." Her voice echoed down the hall. "I won't go into details. Suffice to say, everyone lived."

I cast Bowen a questioning glance. He shrugged

but also made a crooking motion with his finger, signaling me to go stand behind him. When steam began to billow from the back room in thick waves, I obeyed, peeking from around his shoulder.

An odd smell permeated the shop, and then, from out of the vapor, a young woman appeared. She dusted her hands on an apron and used her sleeve to wipe the steam from her brow. Her long brown hair was slightly frizzed at the ends, likely from the steam bath, but her smile was warm and genuine.

She looked nothing like the witch from my nightmares.

"Sorry about the smell... Wow." Her fingers pressed beneath her nose. "How is it worse out here?" Hurrying toward the window, she cracked the pane, letting in a stream of blessedly fresh air. "Anyway, welcome to my shop. What can I do for you? Are you here for magic or murder, because I'm open for both at the moment? Though I do apologize—I'm in a bit of a rush today. I'm attending a magical summit with my best friend, so if you want to make an appointment and come back, that works too."

When she paused for a breath, I broke in. "Actually, I think I met your friend last night. Vivian James, right? That's why we're here."

Tessa's jaw dropped, and her gaze darted between the two of us. "Wait. You're Liana Archer, the woman who helped Viv escape? The one living with Bowen the Beast?"

I made a little clearing noise in the back of my throat. Tessa wasn't nearly as rude as the headmistress from the orphanage, but I was officially putting an end to that nickname. "It's *Bowen MacKenzie*, and yes, that's me."

"Oh, right." She gave Bowen an apologetic smile. "Sorry about that. That's a pretty dreadful nickname, and believe me, I've had my fair share of those. It's no fun. Kids used to call me Tess the Mess until I figured out a spell that made their skin itch until it bled." She made a face and rubbed her arms through her sleeves. "It's as awful as it sounds. But so was the nickname."

I bit my lip to keep from smiling at her antics and realized all my nerves were gone. The scariest thing in the shop was probably the smell wafting from the back room. There were no cages, no sickly-sweet mints, no cruel laughter. I breathed in relief, instantly regretting the act when the lingering smell filled my lungs.

Coughing lightly to clear the smell, I said, "Vivian mentioned if I ever needed a favor, I should come find her or you. The thing is, we're looking for information about a witch and figured you might be the best person to ask."

"A witch, huh? Weird. You're not the first person today to ask me about a witch. Argus Ward was in here earlier too, asking about blood magic. Seems he's interested in a witch as well."

Bowen bristled beside me, but I placed a hand on his arm. "Does that mean you'll help us?"

She waved a hand through the air dismissively. "Of course! Viv made you a promise, and anyone who helps my friend gets my help in return. I won't even charge you my usual fee." Tessa scratched the back of her neck, looking a little sheepish. "I do take tips though. Every bit helps when you're headed to a magical summit. The prices there will make your head spin, and I have my eye on a pretty fancy jar of crystals."

Bowen chuckled and reached into his jacket pocket. The bag of coins thumped against the worktable, crushing a sprig of herbs. "I'm sure we can make it worth your while. Get two jars."

Tessa's eyes went wide. "Now, that's how you negotiate. My partner is super stingy. I mean, I love him, but it's always a big deal when we're handling vendors."

Bowen flashed me an "I told you so" look while Tessa made a quick count of the coins and tried to muffle her squeal of delight.

"So what do you want to know? I'm an open book, and anything I don't know—" Her gaze shifted toward the bookcase, and her lips quirked. "We'll open a book."

I twisted my hands together, trying to find the right explanation without having to go into detail about my past. "I'm sure you've heard of magic vessels, correct?"

"You mean, a person who can move magic from one place to another?"

"Exactly."

"Sure. They're pretty rare, but there's always a few lurking around, hiding in plain sight. At least, the ones who know about their ability. It's not symptomatic until they come into contact with magic." Tessa's focus lowered to my wrist where my birthmark peeked out from beneath my sleeve, but she didn't comment on it.

"That's right. My question has to deal with why a witch would want to use one. They have their own magic. It doesn't make sense to me."

Tessa folded her arms across her chest and leaned against the worktable. "Well, it's fairly simple. You're right, witches have their own magic, but to varying degrees. Sure, we can learn new spells and try different things, but we're really only as powerful as we are to start with. Unless there's a stronger source of magic and a vessel to transfer it. If a witch was looking to grow her power, that would be the way."

My breath caught in the back of my throat. "If that's the case, why would a witch want someone else besides the vessel? She always takes two."

Tessa's brow arched at my slip of the tongue, but again, she let the revealing detail go unquestioned and simply answered, "Amplification."

"What?"

"Look..." Tessa pushed away from the table and paced the floor. "This witch is obviously dealing with an exceptionally potent power source. If she wanted to transfer that magic to herself, a vessel alone wouldn't be strong enough. That's why she needs two. While there is usually only one vessel in a single family, siblings or other close contacts—frankly, anyone the vessel has a strong connection with—can act as an amplifier. It's extremely risky to the amplifier because they're not built for magic to run through them at such a high intensity. It could potentially kill them."

I inhaled a shuddering breath, realizing for the first time Hendrik's role in our captivity. A wave of anger burned in my stomach. She'd meant to use me and sacrifice him, and she planned to do the same with Annie and Ethan. Unless we stopped her.

We will stop her.

"I have one more question." The words scraped the back of my throat, and it almost hurt to ask. "Anyone left behind…for years. Would the witch—?"

"Have them under her control? I'm afraid so. She'd use a spell of some sort, likely causing them to forget those around them and the memories from their life. In a way, I suppose that's almost a blessing if you think about it."

I jerked my head, unable to speak anymore around the tightness in my throat. Bowen squeezed my hand and took over.

"Thank you. That's extremely helpful information. If you can think of anything else that might be relevant…?"

Tessa gave me a solemn look and moved closer. She leaned in, placing her hand on my shoulder, and said, "Always remember that whatever a vessel can give, they can also take."

A little jolt of magic passed through me, and I felt it gather underneath my skin.

Tessa removed her hand and shook out her fingers. She winked and moved back toward the table, noticing a timepiece perched near a glazed pot. Cursing, she finger-combed the frizzy strands of her hair and winced when her fingers got stuck in a tangle.

"I'm so sorry, but I have to run. Vivian's waiting for me, and we cannot miss our ride to the magical summit. The invitation is very specific about arriving at your scheduled time, and you really don't want to anger a supernatural being." She scooped up the bag of coins Bowen had offered and gestured toward the door. "Feel free to make an appointment for when I return if you have any other questions. Oh, and if you ever need any advice in regard to murder, I'm taking appointments for that too."

I cracked a smile. "Well, let's hope that's never the case."

She shrugged. "You'd be surprised. Good luck, you two. I hope you find who you're looking for, and I hope you make her pay."

Chapter 24

Bowen

My stick of charcoal scratched against the parchment as I shaded in a series of shadows beneath the manor's new front entrance. I'd been drawing more and more over the past week and had recently started a new series of plans for the manor. It was time to repair the broken structure and give it one of Liana's trademark overhauls.

At the very least, it was a good distraction from our other problems.

We'd spent the days after meeting with Tessa keeping up our searches and making the rounds in the market district. But it had gone quiet. There were no more sightings of Hendrik or Ethan, which had me worried, and at the same time, slightly relieved. More than anything, I wanted Liana to find her brother and put an end to the witch's grip on their lives and those around us, but a small part of me savored this time we had together.

There was no guarantee it wouldn't come to an end once we dealt with Liana's past. I'd like to think she'd want to continue living at the manor, but there was always the chance she'd return home, back to the life she left behind to come work for me.

So while we waited, I worked on the plans, trying to come up with subtle ways to tempt her to stay.

Leaning back in my chair, I stretched my shoulders and surveyed the piece. Did it make sense to add another glass-enclosed room, this time on the ground level? Maybe a conservatory with a view overlooking the cliff? I made a note on the drawing and sketched out a quick outline.

"What are you doing?" Liana asked from the doorway. Both her hands were hidden behind her back, and her lips were pressed into a mischievous line, suggesting a secret.

"Working on the plans for the manor. But you're just in time. I need a break."

A smile spread across her face as she entered the room and placed the object from behind her back onto my desk. "Well, you're in luck. I have just the thing to distract you. It's almost finished."

My gaze roamed over the crossbow I'd commissioned her to create. She'd designed it to look exactly like my drawing, and it was an almost identical replica to the one I brought back with me on the Incantus mission. Seeing it come to life by her hand was a greater satisfaction than the plans I'd made for my revenge.

"It's amazing." I traced a finger over the bowstring, testing its strength.

"It is. But I thought you'd want to witness the best

part." She set the box of blue flame crystals next to the bow. They glittered in the sunshine cast from the window like icicles refracting light.

I stood and rounded the desk to stand next to her, watching with anticipation as she selected one of the crystals. The blue glow illuminated her features, and she shivered slightly as the magic infused her palms. A thin layer of frost spread up her arm, making a crystal-like pattern over her skin.

"It's so cold," she whispered, and her breath expelled in a white mist.

She drained the crystal of its magic and placed it back on the desk. Her lips were tinged blue, and frost even tipped her eyelashes. She looked like a frozen princess. I couldn't resist touching her cheek. My hand lifted, and she nodded.

"Go ahead. I can control it for a minute or two."

Sliding my palm over her skin, I cupped her jawline. The cold tingle of ice transferred through my fingers.

"Do you feel that?" she asked, leaning into my hand.

"It's like dipping my hand in a frozen lake. You can control the magic?"

She chuckled, exhaling more white mist. "Barely. It wants to flow through me, but I can hold it back just a little."

"Well, hold on for another minute." I lowered my mouth to hers, capturing her lips in a frozen kiss. She moaned into my mouth, letting a little too much magic slip past, and I felt the cold seep through my body. I shivered, stroking my tongue against hers.

The iciness grew stronger the longer we kissed, and my heart slowed to a sluggish beat. I drew deeply on her lips, craving her more with each second, yet knowing we had to stop.

She pulled back, and our frozen breaths mingled. Her eyes, which were normally a forest green, had turned an arctic blue. I could have stared into them forever, but I reached for the crossbow and placed it into her hands, knowing she needed to let the magic go.

Her eyes drifted shut as the ice magic flowed from her body and into the weapon, consolidating in the glass cylinder at the base of the arrow track. Blue flame flickered beneath the glass, and the weapon was complete.

When her eyes opened again, they were green, and the frost coating her skin had melted. She flashed me a seductive grin.

"Well, I can honestly say, I've never kissed someone with magic inside me before. I liked it. A lot."

"Hmm..." My fingers sifted through her hair. "I'm getting lots of ideas for new weapons. Maybe something with fire next time?"

A bubble of laughter escaped her throat, and she danced out of my reach, holding the magical crossbow in the air. "Are you going to hire me for another commission? You should know, my rates have skyrocketed. I saw how much money you gave Tessa. I'll expect double. Triple!"

I grinned in return even though there was a

tightness constricting my chest. What would I have to offer to get her to stay indefinitely, regardless of a commission?

"I'm sure we can come to some sort of a deal. Think about what you'd want."

Her expression sobered, and her gaze held mine. "I will."

Clearing my throat, I drew in a breath and stepped away from the desk. "Jacob and Annie should still be down at the beach with Gavin. Let's go and try out the crossbow. I think Annie will get a kick out of freezing a wave."

***

We made our way down the path, hearing the crash of waves long before we saw them. I had the crossbow strapped to my back, and I couldn't wait to show the others how it worked. It felt as if something years in the making had finally come to fruition, and the last horrible piece of my past had faded away, replaced by the object that had been stolen from me.

The air was bitingly cold even though the sun beamed in the cloudless sky. A salty breeze whipped the hood of Liana's cloak, unleashing her blonde hair to the wind. She paused at the bottom of the path, lifting her hand to shield her eyes from the sun. Searching the shoreline, she craned her neck to see beyond the rocky inlet.

"Where are they?" she asked.

"Maybe Gavin took them around to the other side where the water is a bit calmer." An uneasy feeling spread through my body as we crossed over to the other side. The water lapped lazily against the sand in the shielded cove, but there wasn't any sign of Annie, Jacob, or Gavin.

"Annie!" Liana shouted, her voice carrying away on the wind.

I cupped my hand around my mouth and shouted for Gavin. No one answered. The uneasy feeling thickened, becoming a knot in my stomach.

"Do you think they went back to the manor and we missed them?" Liana asked, stepping on top of a rocky ledge.

I steadied her arm as she peered around the side of the cliff into another inlet. She gasped and nearly toppled off the rock. I caught her around the waist, but she'd already squirmed out of my grip and clambered around the corner.

"Bowen, over here!" She fell to her knees in the sand beside the unconscious forms of Gavin and Jacob. Water licked at their heels, soaking through their clothes. She smoothed the hair from Jacob's face and tried to wake him.

He groaned and winced against the bright sun streaming into his face. I crouched down next to Gavin and roused him, helping him to sit up. He shook his head, pressing the heels of his hands into his eyes.

"How long have we been out?" he croaked.

"We don't know! Where's Annie?" Liana climbed to her feet, searching the small inlet, but the little girl was nowhere to be found.

Jacob shivered. His lips had turned gray. Both of

them needed to get indoors and warmed as soon as possible before hypothermia set in.

Teeth chattering, Jacob tried to speak. "I remember what happened to Annie. We were drawing in the sand, and this strange cloud moved over the sun. It got so dark. That's when we saw the strange woman. She was dressed all in black and had long, stringy hair."

"Why can't I remember?" Gavin asked, blinking the sand and salt from his eyes.

"She did something to you," Jacob said. "Her eyes glowed, and then so did yours. You fell to the ground. Annie started screaming, but then she got real quiet. I tried to stop her, but I couldn't move. She started to walk toward the woman, and then a man appeared. It was the same man from Bowen's drawing."

"Hendrik?" Liana asked.

"Yes. He took Annie's hand, and the two of them left. But the witch stayed behind. I couldn't move, and she came right up to me and whispered something in my ear."

"What did she say?" I demanded, placing both hands on Jacob's shoulders.

"That Liana needed to come too. She gave me this." He unfurled his hand to reveal a small pink mint. "She said it would show you the way and that you needed to come alone."

Liana choked on a sob and stared at the candy in Jacob's palm. She took it from him and closed her fist around it.

I stood and paced a distance away, staring out at the sea. My mind raced, and panic climbed my throat, making it hard to breathe. The witch had Annie. Fists clenched, I tried to think. We had to go after her, but we needed a plan. There was no way in hell Liana was going alone, but it would have to be just the two of us. Any more, and there was a greater risk we'd alert the witch.

Liana came up behind me. "Bowen, look. I've seen those symbols before, haven't I? In your drawings?"

She pointed to a spot in the sand a few feet away. It must have been where Annie was playing because a stick lay on its side next to a series of symbols. I blinked, unable to believe what I was seeing. How was it possible? Had Annie seen my drawings? But then the realization washed over me, and I discovered the truth had been hiding in plain sight this whole time.

My past came roaring back like rolling thunder in my ears.

Robert Lennox had hired me to find the Incantus, but it hadn't been for him. He'd consulted a witch about his ailing health, and she wanted the Incantus as payment. Now, as I stared at the Incantus symbols etched into the sand, I understood there weren't two witches; only one. Liana and Hendrik had been taken years ago by the same witch who played a part in my downfall.

And, according to Tessa, the witch wanted a vessel to transfer the magic from the Incantus medallion into her. Which meant she'd somehow found it after it vanished in the warehouse fire.

Liana murmured beside me, staring at the symbols in the sand. "It makes sense now. When she had us captive, I knew she was searching for something. I didn't know what or even why, but I would sometimes hear her ranting through the walls about not being able to find it. She claimed she'd hired fools." Her gaze found mine. "Bowen, the magic medallion you were hired to find is what she was looking for, isn't it?"

"Yes, I believe so."

"And if she took Annie, it means she probably has it." Liana peered at the mint in her palm. "If the witch wants me, maybe Annie isn't strong enough even with amplification—or who knows? Maybe the witch doesn't want any loose ends. Either way, I have to go after her and Hendrik."

I gripped Liana by the shoulders, forcing her gaze away from the mint and up to mine. "*We're* going after her. Together. Let's get Gavin and Jacob back inside. We'll need supplies, and then we're leaving immediately." I looked overhead at the midday sun. "I want to get there before dark."

Chapter 25

Bowen

We stood at the edge of the forest.

Liana rested her palm on the hilt of her concealed dagger, staring into the gaps between the trees. Shadows gathered where sunlight couldn't seep through the branches, and a thin layer of snow coated the ground.

"Are you sure this is going to work?" she asked, eyeing the crossbow slung over my shoulder. I also had a blade sheathed at my waist and an extra one strapped to my ankle.

"It's as good a plan as any. After you take the mint, I'll follow you at a distance until we reach the cabin."

"And then you're going to free Annie and her brother? That's the most important thing. Whatever I do or wherever I go, you promised you'd get them first."

"I promise. But I'm not leaving without you and Hendrik."

A strangled laugh slipped past her lips. "Good. I don't want to be left behind."

"Never." I framed her face with my hands and made

her look at me. "We go into the woods together, and we come out together. That's the deal."

Liana wrapped her arms around my neck. Leaning forward, she sealed our bargain with a kiss, and I felt her lips tremble against mine. I tried to show her everything would be okay, tried to pour everything I felt for her into that kiss, but it was over too soon.

I brushed the hair off her face, smoothing my fingers down her cheekbones. "Are you ready?"

She removed the small mint from her pocket and held it in her hand. "I swore I'd never eat one of these again. I hate these things, but if it will lead me to her, then I take it gladly." Her gaze tracked back to the forest and she whispered, "I'm coming for you." Closing her eyes, she popped it into her mouth.

A few moments passed while we waited for the mint to take effect, then her whole body tensed. Another minute passed before muscle by muscle, she relaxed, almost going limp in my arms. I held her close while she finished the mint, murmuring words of encouragement I wasn't sure she could hear.

Slightly woozy, her eyes came back into focus, but there was a strange sheen in them. Magic tainted her irises making them glow silver instead of their usual moss-green hue.

"Liana?"

She didn't answer. Slipping out of my arms, she turned toward the forest and started walking almost as if she were asleep, except her eyes were open, and she weaved around every obstacle.

I let her walk until the trees swallowed her up, then

I began following her tracks. We walked for a couple of miles, and I calculated the time left before dark. I wanted them all out of the woods before the sun set. Worst-case scenario, we'd have to find our way in the dark. I'd come prepared with a couple of flares just in case, but I didn't want to rely on them.

The trees were endless, a maze of barren branches and thick swaths of pine. My boots crunched through the thin crust of snow, but there weren't any other sounds as if the closer we got, the witch's power swallowed them all up. There was a loneliness to these woods. An isolation that sank into your bones, making you feel like you might never find your way out, that you might be lost forever.

Her tracks continued as the forest grew thicker.

It was strange, walking this path where our pasts had intersected. I never could have imagined we were connected by a string of circumstances that appeared random until we looked closer. Ever since she'd asked for my help, Liana's fight had become my own, but now, with crystal clarity, I realized it was probably always meant to be this way.

Hadn't I felt a pull the first time I ever heard her name? A connection the moment I saw her face? I might never fully understand why what happened to me did, but in a strange twist, it was another thing I was grateful for. And that was a heavy dose of irony. Grateful for my scars? No. But grateful we were still on the same path, getting closer with each day.

In the distance, I spotted a small clearing. Liana hesitated, still in the shadow of the trees, before continuing closer to the front of an A-frame cabin. Smoke curled from a stone stack set into the roof, and another section of the cabin branched off to the left. A large stack of firewood rested next to a water well and hanging bucket, and I crept closer and crouched behind the well.

The cabin looked unassuming, the perfect spider trap for lost souls.

I knew the moment the fog from the mint lifted when she shook her head and rubbed her eyes. She swiveled her head, looking up into the tree branches and then deep into the forest, likely searching for any sign of me. There was a calmness in her gaze, a fortitude that made me proud. She'd come a long way, and now, not even the shadows could hold her back.

The front door opened, and Hendrik stood in the entrance. I ducked beneath the edge of the well, counting the seconds until I peered around the side again. She faced her brother, neither of them moving. It was a tense moment, each of them seeing each other for the first time in years. Her fingers flexed, trembling slightly, but she stayed still. He didn't seem to recognize her, but he stepped back, using his arm to gesture her inside.

Her feet remained rooted in place as she stared into the gaping darkness of the doorway. I wanted to pull her back, find some other way to draw the witch to us instead of making her walk back into that house. But she squared her shoulders, head held high and stepped forward, following him into the cabin. The door closed tightly behind them.

I stayed where I was even though everything inside me wanted to rush into the house. I counted out the minutes, each second elongating the torturous wait. When I saw the curtain move and a pair of eyes peer into the yard, I knew I'd made the right decision. They were trying to confirm whether she'd come alone. The longer I waited, the more at ease they'd become.

Leaving the well and skirting around the edge of the property, I located the back of the cabin. The windows were covered with grime, so I couldn't see inside. I wasn't sure where they were keeping Annie and her brother, but I had to find a way in.

The back door was boarded up, and even if got through the padlock, there was no way I could remove the boards without anyone hearing. I tried the windows, but they were sealed shut. I rubbed my palms together, trying to think of another way. How would I have breached a hidden temple? The front was usually a trap, the back sealed tight. But there was always another way...

My gaze roamed the yard, looking for anything out of the ordinary, and that was when I spotted the strange object poking out of the ground.

I crept closer, brushing snow off the wooden hatch. It was also padlocked, but I had the tools to pick the lock. Quickly, I set to work, sliding the pins until I heard the soft snick of the lock opening. I lifted the hatch a few inches and held my breath, listening for any sounds inside the dark cavity.

There was only silence.

Slipping inside, I climbed down the nearly rotten

ladder and into the chamber of a root cellar. A scented wave of spoiled vegetables mixed with the aroma of loose dirt assailed my senses. With the little light from the hatch above, I squinted, trying to make out my surroundings.

Rows of shelves lined with glass jars took up one wall, but the other side was in complete darkness. I moved slowly, using my hands as a guide. My eyes adjusted enough that I could see the faint outline of a different ladder leading up to another hatch.

A way in.

I closed the original hatch and then hurried up the other ladder, sending up a prayer this one wouldn't be padlocked from the other side. Thankfully, it wasn't, and I lifted it inch by inch. The hinge whined, and I froze, taking a moment to listen for any sound I'd been discovered.

None came.

The air was dry and hot as I climbed through the hatch and into a narrow hallway. All my instincts came back, and it felt as if I were navigating the tunnels, searching for treasure while avoiding any of the hidden traps. I moved silently on the balls of my feet toward a door at the end of the hall. I could hear voices somewhere deeper inside the house. The low croon of an older woman, and Liana's distinctive tone.

Mere minutes inside the cabin, and the heat was already making the clothes stick to my skin. Sweat beaded on my brow and rolled down the side of my face. I reached the door and pressed my ear against the wood, then I tested the handle.

It wasn't locked.

A child's voice sounded from the other side, and I recognized Annie's soft-spoken tone. I slipped inside, pressing a finger to my lips when I spotted Annie behind a set of metal bars. Her brother sat next to her.

"Bowen, you came for us! I knew you would. I told my brother, didn't I, Ethan? He didn't believe me." Her hushed voice filled the space as she leaped to her feet and wrapped her slender fingers around the bars.

"Shh, Annie. We can't risk anyone hearing us. You have to be totally quiet."

"Yes, sir. I'll be a mouse," she whispered close to my ear as I bent to work the lockpick inside the lock.

"Good girl."

At the sound of my voice, her eyes widened, and she thrust her finger against her lips as if I weren't the one to tell her to be quiet. Ethan moved to stand behind her, watching as I removed the lock and carefully opened the door.

Once it was wide enough, Annie launched through the opening and wrapped her arms around my neck. She kept her promise, not saying a word, but she didn't have to. She squeezed me with every last ounce of strength she had. I picked her up, still clinging to my neck, and waved Ethan forward.

"We're going back out into the hallway and down through the root cellar. Try to stay near the wall where the floorboards won't creak as much. Go slow."

Ethan nodded and followed close behind as we crept out of the room. Flickering shadows danced over the walls from intermittent sconces, and it was difficult to tell what was from a flame and what was a person approaching.

We made it to the hatch, and I sent Ethan down first, then I followed with Annie. With the hatch closed over our heads, I breathed my first sigh of relief. We were going to make it, and then I was keeping my promise to Liana and getting us all out of this nightmare.

"All right, just one more hatch," I whispered. "This is the plan. Once we're outside, Ethan, I want you to take your sister into the woods. Work your way around until you can see the front of the house but you're still in the tree line. I tied a string around one of the trees where there's a good cover, and I want you both to hide until Liana or I come to get you." My gaze focused on Ethan. "If it starts to get dark and we haven't come yet, take your sister and follow the marked trees. They will lead you out of the forest. Go to MacKenzie Manor, and my friend Gavin will help you. Do not under any circumstances come back to this house. Do you understand?"

"Yes, sir. I understand." The boy reached for his sister, but she clung tighter. I gave her a little bounce until she leaned back and peered up at me.

"Go with your brother. Liana and I will be right behind you."

She sniffled but put on a brave face. "We're going home with you, right?"

My throat constricted, but I spoke around the thickness. "Yes, we're going home together. I promise."

Annie took her brother's hand, and he led her up the ladder into the back yard. They kept their heads low until they'd made it to the tree line, where Ethan gave me a signal before they moved deeper into the shadows.

All that was left was to rescue Liana and try to help Hendrik.

I went back the way I came, exiting out into the hallway. Following the voices, I made my way toward the front of the house. The three of them stood in a small parlor. Hendrik was at the witch's side, while Liana faced them both. In front of her, on a wooden table, rested a jeweled box with the lid removed. Inside was the Incantus medallion.

I only felt hatred at seeing it again. That treasure had cost me so much. It had cost us all, and it might still do irreparable damage. It needed to be destroyed, and I wished I'd had the foresight years ago to make that happen. I wished I'd never brought it home.

The witch's throaty voice sounded through the room. "The little girl isn't strong enough on her own, even with her brother, so the task falls to you. It's fitting, isn't it, after all these years? You thought you escaped." She stepped forward and lifted her bony hand. Her nails were black and pointed like claws as they hovered in the air near Liana's chin. "I missed you, child, but thankfully, I've had your brother by my side. Ever since you left him behind."

Liana flinched and turned her gaze to Hendrik. He stood motionless like a puppet, waiting for the witch to pull his strings.

"He waited for you. Every day. In the dark. Until I took all his fears away and made him forget you ever existed." She leaned closer and her voice dropped to a husky rasp. "I'm going to do the same to you. And the children? Who knows...maybe I'll eat them."

"You're disgusting," Liana snapped.

The witch's lips curled revealing a set of rotting teeth. She turned to Hendrik. "Fetch the children, bring them here. The three of them together should be enough."

"No!" Liana shouted, putting herself between her brother and the hallway leading to the cages. "I won't use them to transfer the magic."

"It's your choice. If you won't use the children, I'll make you use your brother. Are you really going to sacrifice him after everything you put him through?"

Liana wavered, trying to find a way to stall for time. But there wasn't any time left. I had to set my plan into motion. As far as plans went, this one had a high risk of going south. It was why I hadn't mentioned it to Liana before we left. I'd promised her I would get her and Hendrik out of here, no matter the cost, and while we'd also made a deal that we would be leaving this forest together, I might have to break it.

I stepped from the shadows. "Use me."

The witch jerked her head in my direction, a snarl forming on her lips. "How did he get in here? I told you to come alone!" Sparks of magic spat from her fingers, and I felt my muscles seize as her spell took hold of my body.

Liana moved in front of me and held up her hands.

"He must have followed me here. I didn't know."

The witch released her spell, and I cocked my head, keeping an eye on the magic sizzling in the her hands a few feet away. "If you ask me, this works out in your favor. You heard her. She won't use the children. Instead, Liana can use me to amplify the magic, and you get to keep Hendrik under your spell. Why lose him when you can just get rid of me?"

"Bowen, no!" Liana whirled. She stared at me with horror etched across her features. Her eyes pleaded with me, telling me with their silent intensity this wasn't part of the plan. But she had to realize there was no plan beyond getting her out by any means possible. And I did have an idea…I just couldn't give too much away. The problem was my idea didn't exactly end with me walking out of there.

This was definitely one of those win, lose situations.

The witch scraped one of her nails across her jawline, giving the idea some thought. Her flinty eyes narrowed. "All right. Hendrik, disarm him." She grabbed the medallion from its jeweled box and placed it on the table, where the symbols glittered in the candlelight. "Transfer the magic, and I'll spare the children's lives. Hendrik stays with me, and you go back into the cell. But whatever happens to him"—her menacing gaze shifted toward me—"is all part of the process. Do it now. I've waited long enough."

Hendrik crossed the room as if in a trance. He reached for the crossbow slung over my shoulder, then the knife I had sheathed. I let him pat me down, finding the ankle weapon. Collecting them all, he walked back toward the witch.

Tears glistened in Liana's eyes, and she shook her head as I approached.

"No—I can't do it. I won't." She staggered back a step, nearly bumping the table.

"You have to. Look at me." I cupped the back of her neck, tilting her head till her gaze connected with mine. Leaning forward, I pressed a kiss against the side of her temple and whispered, "Remember what Tessa said. What you give, you can take." I lingered for a second, breathing in her scent, feeling the softness of her hair against my skin. My mouth grazed her ear. "Take it all."

When I pulled back, a flicker of understanding crossed her features, and she gave a subtle nod.

I grabbed her hand, locking our fingers together.

"Remember you promised me you wouldn't die?" she said.

"You either."

Liana hesitated, staring at the gleaming medallion. The witch snarled and slashed her hand through the air. A gust of heated air stormed through the room, rattling the window panes.

"Do it now!"

With a sharp inhale, Liana closed her fist around the medallion. The jolt of magic stole the breath from my lungs. I tried to keep my eyes open, tried to keep her face in my vision, but the magic magnified, growing stronger and stronger between us until I squeezed my eyes shut as fiery pain seared through

JENNA COLLETT

my body.

Chapter 26

Liana

Take it all.

Bowen's voice echoed in my mind. I knew what he wanted me to do; I was just afraid it wouldn't work, and most of all, I was afraid the magic would kill him. The fact he'd appeared in the parlor gave me strength, knowing he'd already gotten Annie and Ethan out. But now we were racing so fast toward this ending, it took everything inside of me not to collapse to the floor in terrified sobs.

Not that I could. Bowen's grip was so tight around my hand there was no getting free.

The magic hummed between us, flowing from the medallion into me. Unlike the ice magic, this was hot—a scorching fire that traveled up my arm and through my whole body. I breathed through the pain, knowing I could handle the amplified magic, but my heart stopped when Bowen's knees gave out and hit the floor. The force of our grip took me with him.

I wanted to scream, and maybe I was. A sound so horrible I couldn't stand it pressed against my ears. Darkness seeped into the corners of my vision, and a familiar wave of panic climbed my throat.

Then, in a blink, the magic capped itself. Bowen's grasp loosened around my hand and dropped away. His eyes were glassy and feverish, and they kept closing, only for him to force them open again. I reached for him, but his skin scalded me, and I jerked my hand away.

I had to finish the transfer. It was the only way I could focus on Bowen.

Climbing unsteadily to my feet, I approached the witch. All of my fear hardened into rage at what she'd stolen from me, from us, from what she still might take. I glanced at Hendrik's vacant eyes, and then over my shoulder at Bowen's ravaged form. They'd each sacrificed so much, but no more.

My entire body glowed as the blistering magic churned inside me. Every nerve ending sizzled. I'd never experienced such a violent source of power. Her gaze overflowed with triumph, and she held out her gaunt hand, waiting for me to take hers in mine.

"Finally," she murmured, almost delirious in her anticipation. "Come closer. Give me what I've searched for. What is mine!"

What I give, I can take.

The words repeated over and over, a mantra I begged to be true. My fingers clasped hers and magic flowed like molten lava between us. She gasped, and then a wicked laugh burst from her lips.

It died when I swept my foot under her leg, taking her down to the floor just like I'd shown Jacob. The witch's eyes went wide, and she struggled beneath me.

I thrust my palm against her beating heart, feeling her body jerk under mine. Her claws dug into my arms, drawing blood, but I held her in place.

The pain returned, but this time, it was because I was pulling magic from the witch. Grounding my other hand into the floorboards, I felt the Incantus magic drain into the wood. I didn't stop there, drawing the witch's magic through my body and diffusing into the ground until it faded into nothing.

She writhed against my hand, growing weaker the more I drained from her, until finally, she stopped moving altogether. Her sightless eyes peered up at the rafters, and the air seized in her lungs. I withdrew every last ounce of her life force from her body, her magic long emptied into the floor and the earth beneath it.

Removing my hand, I fell on my backside, gulping in huge lungfuls of air. My whole body trembled as I gazed at her unmoving form. Dizziness washed over me, and dark spots danced in my vision. It worked. She was gone.

A hand touched my shoulder, and I jumped, looking up into Hendrik's confused features.

"Liana? Are you all right?"

A sob of relief tore through my chest. I pulled him to me, wrapping my arms around his shoulders in a fierce hug. Six long years. Tears streamed down my face, and a rush of words spilled from my lips.

"It's over, Hendrik. She's dead. I'm so sorry it took me so long to come back for you."

I murmured the apology over and over as he

squeezed me tighter. When I leaned back, I studied his features, taking his face into my palms. "You look so different, and yet the same. We've lost so much time. How can you ever forgive me?"

Hendrik's brow creased and he shook his head. "No don't ask that. You promised me you'd come back. You're here now. That's all that matters." His gaze shifted over my shoulder, and the air lodged in my throat as I remembered our reunion had to wait. "Liana, your friend needs help."

I nodded, struggling to my knees and crawling toward Bowen. His body shuddered from the waves of heat coursing through his system. I didn't know what to do! The fever would kill him if we didn't bring it down. We had to get him outside, in the snow. Maybe that would help.

"Hendrik, help me lift him!"

Silence.

Behind me, something moved, but I knew instantly it wasn't Hendrik. An icy shiver snaked down my back and rose the hair on my arms.

No...

My own voice sounded in my mind. *Never assume the witch is dead. They always come back.*

I glanced over my shoulder as the witch gained her feet. She lunged for my throat, arms outstretched, eyes wild with fury. Fear paralyzed my limbs, and I realized I should have gone for my concealed dagger. A scream built in my throat as I fumbled for the hilt. *Too late... Too late!*

A shot rang out. The crossbow arrow struck the

witch in the chest, and she was thrown backward. It lodged deep inside her rib cage, and blood pooled from the wound. I watched in shock as the blood solidified, freezing along with her body. Frost raced over her skin, coating her limbs, turning them rigid.

Hendrik stood over her, holding the blue flame crossbow. He kicked her in the side, and a piece of her frozen dress shattered.

"I think she's really dead this time."

Stunned, I pulled myself from my stupor and moved back to Bowen. "Help me get him outside. And if the witch moves again, shoot her between the eyes."

Hendrik bent to lift Bowen's shoulders, and I grabbed his legs. I was out of breath, and we'd only moved him a few feet. He was so heavy! Feverish, he moaned in pain as we struggled to carry him to the door. The heat radiating from his body nearly burned my hands, but I tightened my hold, staggering through the last steps until we had him outside.

"Place him here, in the snow."

We lowered him to the ground. I bent over him to remove his jacket then worked the buttons on his shirt. Grabbing a fistful of snow, I pressed it against his exposed torso, but it sizzled, melting almost instantly.

I screamed in frustration. This wasn't working! He was getting worse. Bowen's lips moved, and slurred words escaped his throat. Then he grew quiet, his shudders slowly subsiding as the heat ravaged his body.

Tears blurred my vision as I slipped, trying to

gather more snow. Hendrik took hold of my arms, making me lose the white powder. I grappled to get it back, but he shook me until I looked up at him.

"Stop, Liana. It's too late. There's nothing you can do."

"That's not true!"

"It is. The snow isn't cold enough. It's not working. Let him go."

"No!" I shoved Hendrik off me and spun, searching for anything that would help. Maybe the witch still had some magic left. Why did I drain it all out into the floor? That was so stupid! I needed magic. I needed...

"Give me the crossbow."

"What?"

"The blue flame. I can draw the ice magic, and if I'm really careful, I can use it to cool him down."

"Are you crazy? You saw what that thing did to the witch. It froze her solid in seconds flat. You'll kill him for sure."

"You don't understand. I can control it. I think. I mean, I did before." My mind raced, uncertainty making my chest ache. I had the sudden urge to rage at Bowen, demand to know why he risked his life, knowing full well what the magic would do to him. How could he do this? How could he leave me after everything we'd been through?

"Liana, I can see you care for him, but—"

My teeth gritted, and I spoke through the thickness in my throat, "I love him. I have to try. Hand me the crossbow."

A look of understanding passed between us.

Hendrik obeyed, thrusting the weapon into my hands. Without wasting another moment, I closed my fingers over the glass cylinder and withdrew the ice magic from the weapon. Just like it did before, frost crawled up my arm.

"Your lips are turning blue," Hendrik said, his voice laced with worry.

"It's all right. I can handle it. It won't hurt me." When the last of the magic had drained from the weapon, I removed my hand. The blue flame had extinguished inside the cylinder. There wasn't any more magic. I only had one shot at this.

I hurried back to Bowen's side, feet sliding in the snow. His eyes were closed, and I wasn't even sure if he was still breathing. Tears rolled down my cheeks and splattered against his chest as I leaned over him and slowly lowered my hand.

This has to work. Please! This has to work.

My palm rested against his heart, and the heat from his body nearly dragged the ice magic out of me in one gigantic pull. I clung to my control, slowing down the transfer. The frost melted on my arm, and the magic ebbed from my hand. But he didn't move.

He was so still.

"Liana..."

"Wait!"

Hendrik knelt at my side. A light breeze blew through the trees, lifting the hair off my neck and chilling my skin. I closed my eyes and counted. When the last dregs of magic left my body, I held my breath. He still hadn't moved, and panic creeped around the edges of my tattered composure.

"Come on…come on…"

Bowen began to shiver. It started in his shoulders and then moved through his whole body. His temperature eased, dropping with each second. Relief hit me hard as I pulled my hand away, and Hendrik gave me his jacket. I covered him with it, then I brushed the hair off his face, tracing his features with my fingers.

His eyes opened and blinked. The glassiness was gone, the fever broken. He rubbed his arms beneath the jacket, his teeth chattering.

"It's freezing out here. Why are we always doing things in the cold?"

I laughed and helped him to sit up, hardly waiting to wrap my arms around him. I kissed his face, his forehead, his scars, and finally, his mouth. He crushed me against him, dragging me into his lap, and returned the kiss.

"The crossbow is ruined," I murmured against his lips. "I'll make you another. I'll make you a hundred more. I'm just so happy you didn't die."

He captured my face in his hands. "You either."

Digging my fingers into his shoulders, I squeezed until he winced. "I can't believe you did that! What is wrong with you? If I hadn't just brought you back to life, I would seriously stab you right now."

A cocky grin spread across his features. "That's right. Never trust an angry woman with a sword."

"I'm serious! You almost died. What were you thinking?"

The grin slipped from his face, and his thumbs brushed against my temple. "I'd already decided to volunteer before we ever stepped foot into the woods. I knew you'd never use the children to transfer the magic, and I wasn't going to let you lose your brother again. No matter the cost."

"Bowen…I don't know how to thank you."

His gaze held mine, and there was something in his eyes that made my heart pound. "I'll think of what I want." He wrapped his arms around me, lips finding mine, and drew me closer.

Hendrik cleared his throat. "Sorry to break this up, but there are some kids over there who want to make sure he's okay. And I don't know about you, but I really want to get out of these woods."

Leaning back in Bowen's arms, I gazed at the cabin. "What should we do about the witch?"

"Leave it to me. I think I've earned this." Hendrik strode toward the house. He was gone for a few minutes until smoke billowed out the front door and flames began to lick up the sides of the windows. Hendrik returned, crossing over the threshold, and turned to face the house.

We watched it burn.

Bowen tightened his arms around me as the house from my nightmares caved in, the flames shooting into the clearing and the darkening sky.

"Let's go home," he whispered.

"Together. Let's all go home together."

The five of us followed the path out of the woods, and nobody looked back.

Chapter 27

Liana

The ship crested another wave and sent mist spraying into the air. I held onto the railing and stared at the approaching coastline. From this vantage point, the village where I'd spent the past few years of my life looked exactly the same, and yet I felt like a completely different person.

The witch was dead, Hendrik was released from her spell, Annie and Ethan were free, and now it was time I returned home. Sarah and Thomas would be waiting for us on the docks. I'd written to them detailing our arrival and the fact I wasn't returning alone.

A pair of arms wrapped around my middle, and I leaned my head back against a broad chest. Bowen nuzzled my neck and said, "Have I told you lately how terrible this idea is?"

"It's been a few minutes. Tell me again."

"Your parents are going to skewer me with a fireplace poker."

I scoffed and lifted my hand to rub his cheek. "Don't be ridiculous. We have perfectly good daggers inside my workshop—they won't bother with the poker."

"Your words bring me comfort."

Turning in his arms, I linked my hands around his waist. "Stop worrying. My parents will be so busy meeting the other three they probably won't even remember you framed my father, had him sent to prison, then essentially blackmailed their daughter into working for a disreputable beast."

"Well, when you put it that way..."

"And if they do remember—which they won't—I'll simply remind them how you helped me find Hendrik, saved two young orphans, aided me in killing a witch, and nearly died."

"That list does seem to outweigh the first. Definitely lean into the almost dying part. It's very heroic."

"Trust me, everything will be fine. They won't even mention it."

***

Thomas Archer shot dagger eyes at Bowen from over the dinner table. Forks clinked against the dinnerware, and conversation was sparse. After the initial tearful reunion, we'd settled around the table for a meal, and things had devolved from there.

"Pass the turnips, please," Sarah said, forcing a smile on her lips.

Thomas thumped the bowl of turnips in front of Sarah and continued to glare. Bowen coughed into his napkin and mouthed, "I told you so," at me from across the table. His gaze kept darting to the hearth where there was a suspiciously missing fire poker.

The children ate in silence, sensing the mood, and the twins asked to be excused before they'd even finished their meals. Annie and Ethan followed them from the room, excited to have other kids to play with, leaving only the adults at the table.

My gaze landed on Hendrik's empty place setting, and I frowned. I knew I had to be patient and that his adjustment would take time. It was to be expected, but it was hard to watch him struggle. He was no longer under the witch's spell, but a small part of her still lingered. She lurked in his troubled gaze, and in the nightmares that tore him from sleep. One day, she'd fade into oblivion. Because if there was one thing I'd learned, it was that you can shatter the dark with time and happy memories, and sometimes light breaks through from the places you least expect.

Bowen nudged my leg under the table, breaking me out of my thoughts. He angled his head toward Thomas, eyes pleading with me to say something. I stifled a grin. *Poor guy.* He was getting slaughtered.

Clearing my throat, I leaned forward, and in an exaggerated tone, said, "Not only did he rescue Annie and Ethan from the witch, but did I tell you Bowen almost die—?"

"Where's my pocket watch?" Thomas pushed out of his hair and patted his pockets. "Have you seen it? The thing cost me a fortune. It's gold-plated."

"I haven't seen it," Sarah said, taking a sip from her glass of wine. "Maybe you left it on the bureau?"

"No, I had it with me earlier, and now it's gone." His eyes landed on Bowen, and accusation shot through his tone. "Did you take it?"

"What? No! Of course not." Bowen stood, tossing down his napkin when something jangled inside the pocket of his dinner jacket.

"Is that my watch? Empty your pockets this instant!" Thomas charged around the table as Bowen reached into his jacket. His skin turned slightly gray when he removed a gold pocket watch.

He searched my gaze, horror dawning across his features. "Liana, I didn't take it. I swear, I don't know how it got in there. There has to be a mistake."

My lips flattened. I'd heard that one before. "A mistake, hmm?"

Sarah choked on her wine, sputtering red liquid across the table. She gulped in air between her laughter, trying to dab at the tablecloth with her napkin. "I'm so sorry, Thomas. I tried to hold it in. But his face when he found the watch I planted was too much."

Thomas pressed a fist against his lips and tried to stifle his own amusement. "It's all right, dear. I wasn't sure I could last much longer either. I definitely would have cracked once I started chasing him with the poker."

"How could you do this?" I said, darting a glance at each of them as Bowen sank back into his chair, looking relieved and also a little terrorized by my parents. "Don't you know he almost died!" My lips trembled, and I couldn't hold it. I burst out laughing.

Bowen narrowed his eyes on me. "Did you know about this?"

I lifted my shoulders in a sheepish shrug. "Well, it was Thomas's idea, but I thought it would be a good way to break the ice. You were so worried, but it's okay. They forgive you."

Bowen scrubbed a hand over his face and muttered, "Unbelievable. But I guess I deserved that."

Sarah smiled and reached across the table to pat his hand. "We're a little unorthodox in this family, and believe me, we can hold a grudge with the best of them, but we also know people are complex. You helped our daughter. You helped our family, which has grown quite a bit since that last time she was here, and for those things, we thank you." She pushed aside her plate and rose from her chair. "Let's go, Thomas. I think we've pestered the poor man enough for one night, and I know Liana wants to spend some time with him...alone." My mother bent to kiss the top of my head and whispered, "Why don't you show him your workshop?" She squeezed my hand. "Good luck."

***

I paced the length of the room, waiting for Bowen to join me. It had already been ten minutes, and I was starting to think he was punishing me for my participation in Thomas's prank. A knock sounded, and I turned toward the entrance, surprised to find Hendrik standing in the doorway.

"Hey," I said, motioning him to come inside. "We missed you at dinner. I was getting worried, but I figured with all the commotion, you might need some space."

Hendrik flashed me a weak smile and leaned against my workbench. He wore a pair of Thomas's old clothes, but the shirt was a little tight around his shoulders.

"Sorry. This is still a lot to take in. It feels as if I've been sleeping for six years and I just woke up to a life I don't recognize."

"I know. But it will get better—you'll see."

He nodded absently, and I felt a sharp pain around my heart. I had to remind myself of what it was like when I first escaped the witch. The confusion, the survivor's guilt, and mostly, this singular knowledge I didn't know how to begin putting my life back together. He was going through those same things now, and my vague platitudes weren't helpful.

"Actually, forget I said that. It's hard. Every day. We can't undo the past, and it changed us in ways we can't possibly imagine and probably have yet to discover. I won't pretend I know what it was like for you all those years, but I want you to know you're not alone, and I hope you'll tell me about it. When you're ready." I moved to his side and mimicked his pose, resting my head against his shoulder.

"I'm glad you got away," he murmured. "You know that, right? A lot of what I remember is hazy, but I knew deep down that you escaped. I held on to that feeling. It got me through."

I blinked back the wetness that spiked my lashes. "I blamed myself for a long time. It wasn't fair that

I escaped and you didn't, and I felt responsible. I thought you might hate me."

"It wasn't your fault."

"No, it wasn't. But that didn't make it any easier."

He angled his head so it was resting against mine. A comfortable silence filled the space before he said, "Look at this place. My little sister forges magical weapons." Amusement laced his tone. "I always thought you'd end up as a seamstress like our mother."

"Ha! You know I constantly poked myself with the needle instead of the fabric."

"Your very first dagger."

I elbowed him lightly in the ribs. "Very funny. What about you?"

"I don't think I'd be a very good seamstress either."

"Hendrik..."

"I don't have an answer yet. Thomas offered to take me with him on his next business trip. I'm thinking about taking him up on the offer. Maybe see the world a bit."

My heart sank. "You're leaving? But we just found each other again."

"It won't be forever. I need some time to figure things out. Live a little. Go exploring. I've lost six years of my life, and I don't even know who I am anymore. Besides..." His gaze drifted toward the entrance. He lifted a hand toward Bowen who hesitated when he spotted us. "You have your own future ahead of you." Hendrik ruffled a hand playfully through my hair and pushed away from the table. "We'll talk more in the morning."

"Wait! Before you go, I have a request."

Hendrik let out a heavy sigh, but there was a twinkle in his eye. "Let me guess. The song father used to sing to us before bedtime when we were kids."

"It's my favorite."

"Mine too."

He whistled the first bars of the familiar tune, and I smiled. "Goodnight, Hendrik."

"Goodnight, sis."

Nodding at Bowen on his way out, he disappeared into the night.

"Is everything all right?" Bowen asked, still hovering in the doorway.

I rubbed my arms to ward off the night chill. "Hendrik and I were just discussing the future."

"Ah, the future. An important topic." Bowen approached the workbench, but his gaze roamed the room. Stopping beside me, he ran his fingers over the soot-free worktable and rubbed them together. "So this is your workshop? I can see why you redid mine."

I moved around the space, lighting a few more of the hanging lanterns, then I turned to find him studying one of my creations. He hefted the blade, swinging it in an arc, then placed it back on the worktable.

"It's not exactly a blue flame crossbow, is it? Enchanted steel is so boring." I inhaled a breath, watching the way the light played over his features. I was suddenly nervous. We hadn't discussed what came after this trip, and I was starting to think we weren't going to.

He hadn't asked me to stay even though it was what I wanted him to do. Maybe he needed a little more time to get used to things. Before he escorted me home, he'd had a few inquiries from past clients interested in hiring him again, and he'd even been approached by the Ever Gazette to feature some of his artwork. With his revenge in the past and my problems out of his hands, he was starting to discover he had numerous options in front of him. The last thing I wanted was to stand in the way, and it wasn't even just me anymore. I was a package deal now with Annie and Ethan, and he knew that. Asking me to stay was welcoming them both into his home as well.

But if he wasn't going to bring up the topic, I would. I had a card up my sleeve—I just needed to gather the courage to use it.

I pointed to the rolled scroll sticking out of his inside jacket pocket. "Is that another commission?" My voice sounded hoarse to my ears, and my cheeks heated, but I kept going. "You know, before we left to face the witch, you asked me what I wanted in exchange for another commission. I've been thinking about it, and I know what I want."

He leaned back against the worktable and removed the scroll. "It's not."

"It's not what?"

"A commission."

"Oh." The hope in my chest deflated, and I struggled to find the words to recover. If he wasn't going to offer me another commission, maybe this really was goodbye.

"It's a drawing. I want you to have it." He crooked his finger, and my steps were slow, almost as if I were walking through quicksand. So this was a parting gift. Something to remember him by.

I watched through welling tears as he unfurled the scroll and placed candles at each end. He moved behind me, resting his hands on the table, one on each side of me. I felt his warmth against my back and resisted the urge to close the space and lean against him.

My brow creased as I studied the drawing. It was one I'd seen before, when he brought me back to the manor after getting me released from prison. He'd been drawing it then but had mentioned it wasn't finished.

It was finished now.

The scene was of the cove beneath the manor. Waves crashed against the shore and spilled over the rocks. In the center, playing in the sand, was Annie, and I stood beside her, dipping my toes in the water. I was laughing, my face turned up toward the sunshine.

"It's a beautiful drawing," I said, speaking around the tightness in my throat.

He lowered his head, his voice skating past my ear. "When you saw it the first time, I knew something was missing, and then when I saw you two playing on the beach, it was as if the drawing came to life right in front of me. I had to capture it." Moving his hands to my waist, he turned me to face him. His features softened, but a worry line still marred his brow. "The thing is, I don't know if I have the right to ask you to stay with me after what I did to you. After everything you've given me, it doesn't feel like a fair trade. But I'm asking anyway because this drawing was perfectly fine when it was just a landscape, but now you're in it, I don't think I can go back to one where you're not." His hands lifted to frame my face, and his tone deepened. "You make *everything* better. So stay with me because you want to, because you know I've fallen in love with you, and because you want to build your future with me."

I smiled and drew in a shuddering breath. "You know, I had a fancy speech prepared, but you ruined it when you didn't offer me another commission. You asked me to think about what I wanted, and I planned to tell you all I wanted was you, every day for the rest of my life." I heaved a dramatic sigh. "But now, it looks as if I'm going to have to accept your proposal instead." I held out my hand, and his gaze dropped to my wiggling fingers.

His brow rose. "Really, Liana? A handshake?

"Oh, I'm going to give you more than a handshake. I'm going to seal the deal in every way I know how." I wrapped my arms around his neck and leaned up to kiss him. He groaned against my lips, urging my head back with his hands cupped around the base of my neck. We bumped the workbench rattling a set of metal tools.

Well, this is getting out of control, and we don't even have an agreement.

I pulled back, grinning when he ground his teeth in frustration. "Hold on. There's still the matter of the handshake...and the contract. So let's start at the beginning. Do we have a deal, Bowen MacKenzie?"

His hand closed over mine, and he dragged me to him. "We have a deal, Miss Archer."

And so we did.

The marriage contract came later, and I finally got to finish the rest of my story.

The End...Happily.

P.S. The witch never came back.

Thank you!

I hope you've enjoyed reading Bowen and Liana's story! This fairy tale mashup was so much fun to write and holds a special place in my author journey.

I count myself lucky to have such wonderful support from my family, an amazing editor who's not only talented, but thoughtful in her comments, and the best readers any author could ask for.

***

If you would take a moment to leave a review or a rating, I would greatly appreciate it. For an indie author, reviews and ratings help give a book social proof, which is significant in spreading the word about a series.

If you would like to join my newsletter for new release alerts, cover reveals, and deals, you can sign up at my website:

https://jennacollettauthor.wordpress.com/

Thanks for reading!

-Jenna

Books In This Series

Ever Dark, Ever Deadly

Spellbound After Midnight

Wolfish Charms

Stranded And Spellbound

Shatter The Dark